1/17

# Fever Dream

*Riverhead Books*
*New York*
*2017*

# Fever Dream

*A Novel*

SAMANTA SCHWEBLIN

*Translated by Megan McDowell*

RIVERHEAD BOOKS
An imprint of Penguin Random House LLC
375 Hudson Street
New York, New York 10014

Library of Congress Cataloging-in-Publication Data

Names: Schweblin, Samanta, date. | McDowell, Megan, translator.
Title: Fever dream : a novel / Samanta Schweblin ;
translated by Megan McDowell.
Other titles: Núcleo del disturbio. English
Description: New York : Riverhead Books, 2017.
Identifiers: LCCN 2016026585 | ISBN 9780399184598 (hardback)
Subjects: LCSH: Families—Fiction. | BISAC: FICTION / Literary. | FICTION /
Psychological. | FICTION / Horror. | GSAFD: Psychological fiction.
Classification: LCC PQ7798.29.C5388 N8313 2017 | DDC 863/.64—dc23
LC record available at https://lccn.loc.gov/2016026585
p.      cm.

Printed in the United States of America
1   3   5   7   9   10   8   6   4   2

*Book design by Meighan Cavanaugh*

*For my sister, Pamela*

For the first time in a long while, he looked down and saw his hands. If you have had this experience, you'll know just what I mean.

—JESSE BALL, *The Curfew*

*They're like worms.*

What kind of worms?

*Like worms, all over.*

It's the boy who's talking, murmuring into my ear. I am the one asking questions.

Worms in the body?

*Yes, in the body.*

Earthworms?

*No, another kind of worms.*

It's dark and I can't see. The sheets are rough, they bunch up under my body. I can't move, but I'm talking.

*It's the worms. You have to be patient and wait. And while we wait, we have to find the exact moment when the worms come into being.*

Why?

*Because it's important, it's very important for us all.*

I try to nod, but my body doesn't respond.

*What else is happening in the yard outside the house? Am I in the yard?*

No, you're not, but Carla, your mother, is. I met her a few days ago, when we first got to the vacation house.

*What is Carla doing?*

She finishes her coffee and leaves the mug in the grass, next to her lounge chair.

*What else?*

She gets up and walks away. She's forgetting her

sandals, which are a few feet away on the pool steps, but I don't say anything.

*Why not?*

Because I want to wait and see what she does.

*And what does she do?*

She slings her purse over her shoulder and walks toward the car in her gold bikini. There's something like mutual fascination between us, and also at times, brief moments of repulsion; I can feel them in very specific situations. Are you sure these kinds of comments are necessary? Do we have time for this?

*Your observations are very important. Why are you in the yard?*

Because we've just gotten back from the lake, and your mother doesn't want to come into my house.

*She wants to save you any trouble.*

What kind of trouble? I have to go inside anyway, first for some iced tea with lemon, then for the sunscreen. That doesn't seem like she's saving me any trouble.

*Why did you go to the lake?*

She wanted me to teach her how to drive, she said she'd always wanted to learn. But once we were at the lake, neither of us had the patience for it.

*What is she doing now, in the yard?*

She opens the door of my car, gets into the driver's seat, and digs around in her purse for a while. I swing my legs down off the lounge chair and wait. It's so hot. Then Carla gets tired of rummaging around, and she grips the steering wheel with both hands. She stays like that for a moment, looking toward the gate, or maybe toward her own house, far beyond the gate.

*What else? Why are you quiet?*

It's just, I'm stuck. I can see the story perfectly, but sometimes it's hard to move forward. Is it because of the nurses' injections?

*No.*

But I'm going to die in a few hours. That's going to happen, isn't it? It's strange how calm I am. Because even though you haven't told me, I know. And still, it's an impossible thing to tell yourself.

*None of this is important. We're wasting time.*

But it's true, right? That I'm going to die.

*What else is happening in the yard?*

Carla leans her forehead against the steering wheel and her shoulders start to shake a little; she's crying. Do you think we could be close to the exact moment when the worms are born?

*Keep going, don't forget the details.*

Carla doesn't make any noise, but she gets me to

stand up and walk over to her. I liked her from the start, from the day I saw her walking in the sun and carrying two large plastic buckets. She had her red hair pulled back in a big bun and she was wearing denim overalls. I hadn't seen anyone wear those since I was a teenager. I was the one who insisted on iced tea, and I invited her over for *mate* the next morning, and the next one, and the next one, too. Are these the important details?

*We'll know the exact moment from a detail, you have to be observant.*

I cross the yard. When I skirt the pool, I look in the window toward the dining room to be sure that my daughter, Nina, is still asleep, hugging her big stuffed mole. I get into the car on the passenger side. I sit, but I leave the door open and roll the window down, because it's very hot. Carla's big bun is drooping a little, coming undone on one side. She leans against the backrest, aware that I'm there now, beside her once again, and she looks at me.

"If I tell you," she says, "you won't want me to visit anymore."

I think about what to say, something like "Now Carla, come on, don't be silly," but instead I look at her toes, tense on the brakes, her long legs, her thin but strong arms. I'm disconcerted that a woman ten years older than me is so much more beautiful.

"If I tell you," she says, "you won't want him to play with Nina."

"But Carla, come on, how could I not want that."

"You won't, Amanda," she says, and her eyes fill with tears.

"What's his name?"

"David."

"Is he yours? Is he your son?"

She nods. That son is you, David.

*I know. Go on.*

She wipes away her tears with her knuckles, and her gold bracelets jangle. I had never seen you, but when I'd mentioned to Mr. Geser, the caretaker of our rental house, that I'd made friends with Carla, he asked right away if I'd met you yet. Then Carla says:

"He was mine. Not anymore."

I look at her, confused.

"He doesn't belong to me anymore."

"Carla, children are forever."

"No, dear," she says. She has long nails, and she points at me, her finger level with my eyes.

Then I remember my husband's cigarettes, and I open the glove compartment and hand them to her with a lighter. She practically snatches them from my hand, and the perfume of her sunscreen wafts between us.

"When David was born, he was the light of my life, he was my sun."

"Of course he was," I say, and I realize I need to be quiet now.

"The first time they put him in my arms, I was so anxious. I was convinced he was missing a finger." She holds the cigarette between her lips, smiling at the memory, and she lights it. "The nurse said sometimes that happens with the anesthesia, it can make you a little paranoid. I swear, until I counted all ten of his fingers twice, I wasn't convinced everything had turned out all right. What I wouldn't give now for David to simply be missing a finger."

"What's wrong with David?"

"But back then he was a delight, Amanda, I'm telling you: my moon and stars. He smiled all day long. His favorite thing was to be outside. He was crazy about the playground, even when he was tiny. You see how around here you can't go for a walk with a stroller. In town you can, but from here to the playground you have to go between the big estates and the shanties along the train tracks. It's a mess with all the mud, but he liked going so much that until he was three I'd carry him there, all twelve blocks. When he caught sight of the slide he'd start to shout. Where's the ashtray in this car?"

It's under the dashboard. I pull out the base and hand it to her.

"Then David got sick, when he was that age, more or less, about six years ago. It was a difficult time. I'd started working at Sotomayor's farm. It was the first job I'd worked in my life. I did the accounting, which really wasn't anything like accounting. I just filed papers and helped him add, but it kept me entertained. I went around town on errands, all dressed up. It's different for you, coming from the capital, but around here you need an excuse for a little glamour, and the job was the perfect pretext."

"What about your husband?"

"Omar bred horses. Yes, that's right. He was a different guy back then, Omar."

"I think I saw him yesterday when Nina and I were out walking. He drove by in the pickup, but when we waved he didn't wave back."

"Yes, that's Omar these days," says Carla, shaking her head. "When I met him he still smiled, and he bred racehorses. He kept them on the other side of town, past the lake, but when I got pregnant he moved everything to where we are now. Our house used to be my parents'. Omar said that when he hit it big, we'd be loaded and we could redo everything. I wanted to carpet the floors. Yes, it's crazy living where I do, but oh, I really wanted it. Omar had two spectacular mares that had given birth to a couple of big winners. They'd been sold and were running races—still do—at Palermo and San Isidro. Later, two more fillies were born, and a colt; I don't remember any of their names. To do well in that business you have to have a good stallion, and Omar got hold of the best. He fenced in part of the land for the mares, built a corral behind it for the foals, planted alfalfa, and then he could take his time building the stable. The deal was that Omar would borrow the stallion for two or three days, and later, when the foals were sold, a fourth of the money went to the stallion's owner. That's a lot of money, because if the stallion is good and the foals are well taken care of, each of them goes for between 200,000 and 250,000 pesos. Anyway, one time we had that precious horse with us. Omar watched him all day long, followed him around like a zombie to keep track of how many times he mounted each mare. He wouldn't leave the house until I got back from Sotomayor's, and then it was my turn, though I would just take a look out the kitchen window at him every once in a while, as you can imagine. So one afternoon I'm washing the dishes and I realize I haven't seen the stallion in a while. I go to the other window, then to another that looks out behind the house, and nothing: the mares are there, but no sign of the stallion. I pick David up, who by then had taken his first steps and had been following me around the house that whole time, and I go outside. There's only so much searching you can do, either a horse is there or it's not. Evidently, for some reason he'd jumped the fence. It's rare, but it happens. I went to the stable praying to God he'd be there, but he wasn't. Then my eyes fell on the stream and I felt a spark of hope; it's small but it runs in a hollow, a horse could be drinking water and you wouldn't even see it from the house. I remember David asking what was happening. I was still carrying him, he was hugging my neck and his voice was clipped by the long strides I was taking, bouncing him side to side. 'There, Mom!' said David. And there was the stallion, drinking water from the stream. David doesn't call me Mom anymore. We went toward it, and David wanted me to put him down. I told him not to go near the horse, and I went toward the animal, taking short little steps. Sometimes he moved away, but I was patient, and after a while he started to trust me. I managed to get hold of the reins. It was such a relief, I remember it perfectly, I sighed and said out loud, 'If I lost you, I'd lose the house too, you jerk.' See, Amanda, this is like the finger I'd thought David was missing. You say, 'Losing the house would be the worst,' and later there are worse things and you would give the house and even your life just to go back to that moment and let go of the damned animal's reins."

I hear the slam of the screen door from the living room and both of us turn toward the house. Nina is in the doorway, hugging her stuffed mole. She's sleepy, so sleepy it doesn't even scare her when she doesn't see us anywhere. She takes a few steps, and without letting go of the stuffed animal she grabs the railing and concentrates on going down the three porch steps until she's on the grass. Carla leans back in the seat and watches her in the rearview mirror, silent. Nina looks down at her feet. She has a new habit since we got here, and she's doing it now: pulling up the grass by clenching it between her toes.

"David had knelt down in the stream, his shoes were soaked. He'd put his hands in the water and was sucking on his fingers. Then I saw the dead bird. It was very close to David, just a step away. I got scared and yelled at him, and then he got scared, too. He jumped up and fell backward onto his bottom from the fear. My poor David. I went over to him dragging the horse, who neighed and didn't want to follow me, and somehow I picked him up with just one hand and I fought with both of them until we made it back up the hill. I didn't tell Omar about any of it. What for? The screwup was over and done with, fixed. But the next morning the horse was lying down. 'He's not there,' said Omar. 'He escaped,' and I was about to tell him that he'd already escaped once, but then he saw the horse lying in the pasture. 'Shit,' he said. The stallion's eyelids were so swollen you couldn't see his eyes. His lips, nostrils, and his whole mouth were so puffy he looked like a different animal, a monstrosity. He barely had the strength to whinny in pain, and Omar said his heart was pounding like a locomotive. He made an urgent call to the vet. Some neighbors came over, everyone was worried and running back and forth, but I went into the house, desperate, and I picked up David, who was still sleeping in his crib, and I locked myself in my room, in bed with him in my arms, to pray. To pray like a crazy woman, pray like I'd never prayed in my life. You'll be wondering why I didn't run to the clinic instead of locking myself in the bedroom, but sometimes there's not enough time to confirm the disaster at hand. Whatever the horse had drunk my David had drunk too, and if the horse was dying then David didn't have a chance. I knew it with utter clarity, because I had already heard and seen too many things in this town: I had a few hours, or maybe minutes, to find a solution that wasn't waiting half an hour for some rural doctor who wouldn't even make it to the clinic in time. I needed someone to save my son's life, whatever the cost."

I steal another look at Nina, who is now taking a few steps toward the pool.

"It's just that sometimes the eyes you have aren't enough, Amanda. I don't know how I didn't see it—why the hell was I worrying about a goddamn horse instead of my son?"

I'm wondering whether what happened to Carla

could happen to me. I always imagine the worst-case scenario. Right now, for instance, I'm calculating how long it would take me to jump out of the car and reach Nina if she suddenly ran and leapt into the pool. I call it the "rescue distance": that's what I've named the variable distance separating me from my daughter, and I spend half the day calculating it, though I always risk more than I should.

"Once I decided what I would do there was no going back. The more I thought about it, the more it seemed like the only possible way out. I picked up David, who was crying because he could sense my fear, and I left the house. Omar was standing over the horse and arguing with two men, and every once in a while he clutched his head. Two more neighbors were watching from the lot behind us and sometimes jumped into the conversation, shouting opinions from their field to ours. No one noticed when I left. I went out to the street," said Carla, pointing toward the end of my yard and beyond the gate, "and I went to the green house."

"What green house?"

The last ash of her cigarette falls between her breasts and she brushes it away, blowing a little, and then she sighs. I'm going to have to clean the car tomorrow, my husband is very meticulous about these things.

"The people who live around here go there sometimes, because we know that those doctors they call in to the clinic always take hours to arrive, and they don't know anything and can't do anything. If it's serious, we go to the woman in the green house," says Carla.

Nina leaves her stuffed mole on my lounge chair,

on the beach towel. She takes some more steps toward the pool, and I sit up, alert, in my seat. Carla looks too, but the situation doesn't seem to worry her. Nina crouches down, sits on the edge of the pool, and puts her feet into the water.

"She's not a psychic. She always makes sure people understand that. But she can see people's energy, she can read it."

"What do you mean, she can read it?"

"She can tell if someone is sick, and where in the body the negative energy is coming from. She cures headaches, nausea, skin ulcers, and cases of vomiting blood. If you reach her in time, she can stop miscarriages."

"Are there that many miscarriages?"

"She says that everything is energy."

"My grandmother always said that."

"What she does is detect it, block it if it's negative, mobilize it if it's positive. Here in town people consult her a lot, and sometimes people come from out of town to see her. Her children live in the house behind hers. She has seven kids, all boys. They take care of her and see to all her needs, but people say they never go into her house. Should we go over to the pool with Nina?"

"No, don't worry."

"Nina!" Carla calls out to her, and only then does Nina see us in the car.

Nina smiles. She has a divine smile: her dimples show and her nose wrinkles a little. She stands up, picks up her mole from the beach chair, and runs toward us. Carla reaches to open the backseat door for her. She moves in the driver's seat with such naturalness it's hard to believe she got in this car for the first time today.

"But I have to smoke, Amanda. I'm sorry about Nina, but I can't finish this story without another smoke."

I make an unconcerned gesture and hand her the pack again.

"Blow it out the window," I say while Nina gets into the backseat.

"Mommy."

"What, sweetie?" says Carla, but Nina ignores her and asks me:

"Mommy, when are we going to open the box of lollipops?"

Well trained by her father, Nina settles in and buckles her seat belt.

"In a little while," I tell her.

"Okay," says Nina.

"Okay," says Carla, and that's when I notice there's nothing left now of the drama from before she started to tell her story. She's not crying anymore, she's not leaning her head against the steering wheel. She is unbothered by the interruptions as she talks, as if she had all the time in the world and were enjoying this return to her past. I wonder, David, if you could really have changed that much, if for Carla telling it all over again brought her back, if only for a moment, to that other son she claims to miss so much.

"As soon as the woman opened the door I thrust David into her arms. But people like her are sensible as well as esoteric. So she put David down on the floor, gave me a glass of water, and wouldn't start talking until I'd calmed down some. The water brought a little of my soul back to my body and it's true, for a moment I considered that my fears might all be a fit of madness, I thought of other possible reasons why the horse could be sick. The woman was staring at David while he played, arranging the decorative miniatures that were on the TV table into a single-file line. She went over to him and played with him a moment. She studied him attentively, discreetly, sometimes resting a hand on his shoulder, or holding his chin to look him straight in the eyes. 'The horse is already dead,' said the woman, and I swear I hadn't said anything yet about the horse. She said David still had a few hours, maybe a day, but that soon he would need help breathing. 'It's poison,' she said. 'It's going to attack his heart.' I sat there looking at her. I don't even remember how long I was like that, frozen and unable to say a word. Then the woman said something terrible. Something worse than announcing to you how your son is going to die."

"What did she say?" asks Nina.

"Go on inside and open the lollipops," I tell her.

Nina takes off her seat belt, grabs her mole, and runs toward the house.

"She said that David's body couldn't withstand the poisoning, that he would die, but that we could try a migration."

"A migration?"

Carla puts out her unfinished cigarette and leaves her arm outstretched, almost hanging from her body, as if the whole exercise of smoking had left her completely exhausted.

"If we could move David's spirit to another body in time, then part of the poison would also go with him. Split into two bodies, there was the chance he could pull through. It wasn't a sure thing, but sometimes it worked."

"What do you mean, sometimes? She'd done it before?"

"It was the only way she knew to save David. The woman handed me a cup of tea, she said that drinking it slowly would calm me down, that it would help me make my decision, but I gulped it down in two sips. I couldn't even put what I was hearing in order. My head was a tangled mess of guilt and terror and my whole body was shaking."

"But do you really believe in those things?"

"Then David tripped, or it seemed to me he'd tripped, and then he didn't get up. I saw him from behind, wearing his favorite shirt that had little soldiers on it, trying to coordinate his arms so he could stand up. It was a clumsy and futile movement that reminded me of the ones he'd made when he was still learning to stand on his own. It was an effort he didn't need to make anymore, and I understood that the nightmare was starting. When he turned toward me he was frowning, and he made a strange gesture, like he was in pain. I ran to him and hugged him. I hugged him so hard, Amanda, so hard it seemed impossible that anyone or anything in the world could take him from my arms. I heard him breathing very close to my ear, a little fast. Then the woman separated us with a gentle but firm movement. David sat back against the sofa, and he started to rub his eyes and mouth. 'We'll have to do it soon,' said the woman. I asked her where David, David's soul, would go, if we could keep him close, if we could choose a good family for him."

"I don't know if I understand, Carla."

"You do understand, Amanda, you understand perfectly."

I want to tell Carla that this is all a bunch of nonsense.

*That's your opinion. It's not important.*

It's just that I can't believe a story like that. But at what point in the story is it appropriate to get angry?

"The woman said that she couldn't choose the family he went to," said Carla. "She wouldn't know where he'd gone. She also said that the migration would have its consequences. There isn't room in a body for two spirits, and there's no body without a spirit. The transmigration would take David's spirit to a healthy body, but it would also bring an unknown spirit to the sick body. Something of each of them would be left in the other. He wouldn't be the same anymore, and I would have to be willing to accept his new being."

"His new being?"

"To me it was so important to know where he would go, Amanda. But she said no, it was better not to know. She said the important thing was to free David from the sick body, and to understand that, even without David in that body, I would still be responsible for it, for the body, no matter what happened. I had to accept that compromise."

"But David . . ."

"And while I was turning it all over in my mind, David came up to me again and hugged me. His eyes were swollen, his eyelids were red and taut, inflated like the horse's. He wasn't exactly crying—the tears were falling but he didn't shout or blink. He was weak and terrified. I kissed his forehead and I realized he was burning with a high fever. Burning up, Amanda. At that moment my David must have already been seeing heaven."

Your mother grabs the steering wheel and sits looking at the gate at the end of my driveway. She is losing you all over again: the happy part of her story is over. When I met her some days before, I'd thought she was renting a summerhouse like I was, while her husband was working nearby.

*What made you think she was from out of town, too?*

Maybe because I saw her as so sophisticated, with her colored blouses and her big bun, so nice, so different and foreign from everything around her. Now I feel uneasy because she starts crying again, and because she won't let go of the wheel in my husband's car, and because Nina is wandering around the house alone. I should have told Nina that when she got the lollipops she should come back to the car, but no, better for her to stay away, there's no reason for Nina to hear this story.

"Carla," I said.

"I told her yes. I told her to do it. I said we should do whatever we had to do. The woman wanted us to go into another room. I picked up David, who practically passed out on my shoulder. He was so hot and so swollen he felt strange to the touch. The woman opened the door to a room, the last one at the end of the hall. She gestured to me to wait in the doorway, and she went in. The room was dark, and from outside I could barely make out what she was doing. She put a large, low washbasin in the center of the room. I understood what it was when I heard the sound of the water, which she poured into a bucket first. She went out to the kitchen, looking focused as she passed us, and halfway there she turned and looked at David for a moment. She looked at his body as if she wanted to memorize his shape or maybe his measurements. She came back with a big spool of thin hemp rope and a handheld fan, and she went back into the room. David was boiling so much by then that when she took him from me my neck and chest were soaked with sweat. It was a quick movement, her hands darted out from the room's darkness and then disappeared again with David. It was the last time I held him in my arms. The woman came out again, without David; she led me to the kitchen and poured me more tea. She said I'd have to wait right there. If I moved around the house, she said, I could shift other things by accident. In a migration, she said, only the things that are prepared to move should be in motion. And I clutched the teacup and leaned my head against the wall. She went back down the hall without another word. At no point did David call for me, nor did I hear him talk or cry. A few minutes later, I heard the door to the bedroom close. On a kitchen shelf across from me, the seven sons, now grown men, stared out at me the whole time from a large picture frame. Naked from the waist up, red beneath the sun, they were smiling and leaning on their rakes, and behind them was the big soy field, recently cut. And just like that, motionless, I waited for a long time. Maybe two hours, I'd say, without drinking the tea or ever taking my head from the wall."

"Did you hear anything, in all that time?"

"Nothing. Just the door opening once it was all over. I straightened up, pushed the tea aside, my whole body alert, but I couldn't bring myself to get up. I didn't know if I was still capable. I heard her footsteps, which by then I could recognize, but nothing else. The steps stopped halfway to the kitchen, before she came into view. And then she called to him. 'Come on, David,' she said. 'I'm going to take you to your mother.' I held on to the edge of my seat. I didn't want to see him, Amanda, all I wanted was to escape. I wanted it desperately. I wondered if I could reach the front door before they got to the kitchen. But I couldn't move. Then I heard his footsteps, very soft on the wood. Short and uncertain, so different from how my David walked. They stopped after every four or five steps; hers would stop as well while she waited for him. They were almost to the kitchen. His little hand, dirty now with dry mud or dust, fumbled over the wall as he leaned against it. Our eyes met, but I looked away immediately. She pushed him toward me and he took a few more steps, almost stumbling, and now he was leaning on the table. I think I'd stopped breathing for that entire time. When I started again, when he took another step toward me, this time of his own volition, I leaned away. He was very flushed, and sweating. His feet were wet; the damp prints he'd left behind him were already starting to dry."

"And you didn't pick him up, Carla? You didn't hug him?"

"I sat there looking at his dirty hands. He was using them to hold on to the table like a railing as he walked, and then I saw his wrists. He had marks on his skin, lines like bracelets around his wrists, and a little above them, too, maybe left by the rope.

'It seems cruel,' said the woman as she approached, watching my reaction and David's next step, 'but we have to make sure that only the spirit leaves.' She caressed his wrists, and as if forgiving herself she said, 'The body has to stay.' She yawned, I realized she had been yawning since she returned to the kitchen. She said it was the effect of the transmigration, and that it would happen to him, too, as soon as he finished waking up. It was important to get it all out, to yawn with the mouth wide open, to 'let it go.'"

"What did David do?" I asked.

"The woman pulled out the chair next to me for him to sit down."

"And you? You didn't even touch him, poor thing?"

"Then the woman poured more tea, keeping an eye on us while she did, watchful over our meeting.

David had trouble climbing into the chair, but I couldn't bring myself to help him. Then he sat there looking at his hands. 'He has to yawn soon,' said the woman, yawning deeply, covering her mouth. She sat down at the table too, with her tea, and she looked at him attentively. I asked her how it had gone. 'Better than I expected,' she said. The transmigration had taken part of the poison away, and now, split between two bodies, it would lose the battle."

"What does that mean?"

"That David would survive. David's body, and also David in his new body."

I look at Carla and Carla looks at me. She's wearing an openly false smile, like a clown's, which for a moment confuses me and makes me think that this is all a long joke in bad taste. But she says:

"So this one is my new David. This monster."

"Carla, don't get mad, but I need to see what Nina's up to."

She nods and looks back at her hands on the steering wheel. I shift, preparing to get out of the car, but she makes no move to follow me. I hesitate for a moment but now I really am worried about Nina. How can I measure my rescue distance if I don't know where she is? I get out and walk toward the house. There's a bit of a breeze, I can feel it on my back and on my legs, sweaty from the seat. Then I see Nina through the window. She's moving a chair from the living room to the kitchen, dragging it behind her. Everything's in order, I think, but I keep walking toward the house. Everything in order. I go up the three steps to the deck, open the screen door, go in, and close it behind me. I slide the lock because that's what I always do, instinctively, and with my forehead against the screen I stand looking at the car, alert to any movement, watching the red bun above the driver's-seat headrest.

She called you a monster, and I keep thinking about that. It must be very sad to be whatever it is you are now, and on top of that your mother calls you a monster.

*You're confused, and that's not good for this story. I'm a normal boy.*

This isn't normal, David. There's only darkness, and you're talking into my ear. I don't even know if this is really happening.

*It's happening, Amanda. I'm kneeling at the edge of your bed, in one of the rooms at the emergency clinic. We don't have much time, and before time runs out we have to find the exact moment.*

And Nina? If all of this is really happening, where is Nina? My God, where is Nina?

*That doesn't matter.*

It's the only thing that matters.

*It doesn't matter.*

Enough, David, I don't want to keep going.

*If we don't go on, there's no reason for me to stay here with you. I'm going to leave, and you'll be left alone.*

No, please.

*What happens now, in the yard? You're in the doorway, you have your forehead against the screen.*

Yes.

*And then?*

Carla's bun moves a little over the seat, as if she were looking to either side.

*What else? What else is happening in that very moment?*

I shift the weight of my body from one leg to the other.

*Why?*

Because it's a relief; because lately I feel like staying on my feet requires a huge effort. I told my husband about that feeling once, and he said maybe I was depressed. That was before Nina was born. The feeling is still there, but it's not the most important thing now. I'm just tired, that's what I tell myself, and sometimes I'm afraid when I think that everyday problems might be a little more terrible for me than for other people.

*And what happens then?*

Nina comes up to me and hugs my legs.

"What's wrong, Mommy?"

"Shhh."

She lets go of me and leans against the screen door

too. Then the car door opens. One of Carla's legs emerges, then the other. Nina gives me her hand. Carla stands, picks up of her purse, and adjusts her bikini. I'm afraid she's going to turn toward us and see us, but she doesn't; she doesn't even cross the yard to pick up her sandals. She walks directly to the gate with her purse under her arm. Upright and in a straight line, as if she were wearing a long dress that required a lot of concentration when she walked. Only when your mother reaches the street and disappears behind the privet does Nina let go of me. Where is Nina now, David? I need to know.

*Tell me more about the rescue distance.*

It changes depending on the situation. For example, in the first hours we spent in the vacation house, I wanted Nina close by at all times. I needed to know how many exits the house had, find the areas of the floor with the most splinters, see if the creaky stairs posed any kind of danger. I showed these things to Nina, who isn't fearful but is obedient, and on the second day the invisible thread that ties us together unspooled again. It was there, but it was more permissive, it gave us independence, on and off. So, the rescue distance is important?

*Very important.*

I go into the kitchen and Nina follows me. I sit her on a bench and then I make a little salad with tuna. Nina asks me if the woman is gone, if I'm sure, and when I tell her yes she gets down from the bench and goes running outside through the door leading to the yard, and she runs all the way around the house, shouting and laughing, and then she comes back inside. It takes her less than a minute. I call her in and sit her down in front of her plate, she eats a little and then goes out to take another lap around the house.

*Why does she do that?*

It's a routine she's gotten into here. She runs two or three times around the house at every lunch.

*This is important. This could have to do with the worms.*

When Nina passes the kitchen window, she presses her face against the glass and we smile at each other. I like her bursts of energy, but this time her running makes me anxious. My conversation with Carla pulled the rope that ties me to my daughter even tighter, and the rescue distance is shorter again. How different are you now from the David of six years ago? What did you do that was so terrible your own mother no longer accepts you as hers? These are the things I can't stop wondering about.

*But they aren't the important things.*

When Nina finishes her salad we go out to the car together, carrying our empty shopping bags. She gets into the backseat, buckles her seat belt, and starts asking questions. She wants to know where the woman went when she got out of the car; she wants to know where we are going to buy the food, whether there are other kids in town, if she can pet the dogs, if the trees around the house are all ours. She wants to know, especially, she says as she buckles her stuffed mole in too, whether people here speak the same language we do. The car's ashtray is clean and the windows are rolled up. I lower mine, and I wonder when exactly Carla could have gone to the trouble to tidy up the car. A fresh breeze enters with the sun, which is already burning. We're driving slowly and calmly; that's how I like to go, and when my husband drives it's impossible. This is my moment to drive, when I'm on vacation, skirting potholes of gravel and earth between the weekend estates and the locals' houses. In the city I can't drive, the traffic makes me too nervous. You said these details were important.

*Yes.*

Twelve long blocks separate us from downtown, and as we get closer the houses grow smaller and more humble, fighting each other for space, with tiny yards and fewer trees. The first paved street is the boulevard that crosses the downtown from one end to the other, around ten blocks. It's paved, yes, but there is so much dirt that the feeling inside the car as we drive hardly changes. It's the first time we've made this trip, and Nina and I talk about how nice it is to have the whole afternoon ahead of us to shop and think about what we're going to have for dinner.

There is a small market in the main square, and we park the car so we can walk a little.

"Let's leave the mole in the car," I say to Nina.

And she says, "Yes, m'lady," because sometimes we like to put on airs and speak to each other like rich nobility.

"And how would the lady like some candied nuts?" I ask, helping her out of the car.

"We would love some," says Nina, who has always been convinced that lords and ladies speak in the plural.

*I like that, about the plural.*

There are seven stalls improvised using boards and trestles, or just with canvases on the ground. But it's good food, artisanally produced or grown on the local estates. We buy fruits, vegetables, and honey.

Mr. Geser had recommended a bakery where they bake whole-grain rolls—apparently they're famous around here—and we go there, too. We buy three, to give ourselves a real bellyful. The two old men who work there give Nina a doughnut filled with *dulce de leche*, and they almost cry with laughter when she takes a bite and says, "How divine! We adore it!" We ask where we can find a blow-up toy for the pool, and they give us directions to House & Home. We have to go from the other side of the boulevard, some three blocks toward the lake, and since we have energy to spare we drop our purchases in the car and walk there. In House & Home, Nina picks out a killer whale. It's the only one, but she points to it without hesitation, sure of her decision. While I'm paying, Nina walks away. She's somewhere behind me, walking among the appliance display racks and the garden tools; I don't see her, but the rope pulls taut and I could easily guess where she is.

"Can I get you anything else?" the woman at the register asks.

A piercing cry interrupts us. It's not Nina's voice—that's the first thing I think. It's high-pitched and clipped, like a bird imitating a child. Nina comes running from the kitchen aisle. She's flustered, somewhere between amused and scared, and she grabs hold of my legs and stands staring back toward the end of the aisle. The cashier sighs in resignation and turns to come out from behind the counter. Nina pulls on my hand so I'll follow the woman down the same aisle. Ahead of us, the woman puts both fists on her hips, pretending to be angry.

"What did I tell you? What did we talk about, Abigail?"

The cries repeat, clipped but much quieter now, almost shy at the end.

"Come on, let's go."

The woman reaches out her hand toward the other aisle, and when she turns back toward us, a small hand comes with her. A little girl slowly appears. At first I think she is still playing, because she hobbles so much she looks like a monkey, but then I see that one of her legs is very short, it barely goes past her knee, but she still has a foot. When she raises her head to look at us we see her forehead, an enormous forehead that takes up more than half her face. Nina squeezes my hand and laughs her nervous laugh. It's good for Nina to see this, I think. It's good for her to realize that we aren't all born the same, and to learn not to be scared. But secretly I think that if the girl were my daughter I wouldn't know what to do, it would be horrible. Then your mother's story pops into my head. I think about you, or about the other David, the first David without his finger. This is even worse, I think. I wouldn't have the strength. But the woman comes toward us dragging the girl patiently; she wipes her bald head as if it were dusty, and she talks to her sweetly in her ear, saying something about us that we can't hear. Do you know that girl, David?

*Yes, I know her.*

Is there part of you in her body?

*Those are stories my mother tells. Neither you nor I have time for this. We're looking for worms, something very much like worms, and the exact moment when they touch your body for the first time.*

"Who is she, Mommy?"

There's no more put-on nobility now. When they are close to us Nina takes a few steps back; she wants us to move farther away. We make room for them by pressing up against the ovens. The girl is Nina's height but I couldn't say how old she is. I think she's older, maybe your age.

*Don't waste time.*

It's just that your mother must know this girl, the girl and her mother and their whole story. And I go on thinking about Carla as the woman leads the little girl around the counter and the girl disappears from view because of her height. The woman presses the button on the register and hands me the change with a sad smile. She does all of this with both hands, one for the button, the other for my money, and just as I'd wondered a moment before how she could take that child's hand, now I wonder how it's possible to let go of it, and I accept the change thanking her many times, with guilt and remorse.

*What else?*

We go back home and Nina is sleepy. A nap so late is a bad business, later she has trouble falling asleep at night. But we're on vacation—that's what we're here for. I remind myself of that so I'll relax a little. As I put away the food we bought, Nina falls soundly asleep on the living room sofa. I know her sleep. If nothing loud wakes her up, she could be there for at least an hour or two. And then I think about the green house, and I wonder how far away it is. The green house is the house where the woman took care of you.

*Yes.*

The one who saved you from the poison.

*That is not important.*

How can it not be? That's the story we need to understand.

*No, that's not the story, it has nothing to do with the exact moment. Don't get distracted.*

I need to measure the danger, otherwise it's hard to calculate the rescue distance. The same way I surveyed the house and its surroundings when we arrived, now I need to see the green house, understand its gravity.

*When did you start to measure this rescue distance?*

It's something I inherited from my mother. "I want you close," she'd say to me. "Let's stay within rescue distance."

*Your mother isn't important. Go on.*

Now I walk away from the house. It'll be fine, I think. I'm sure the walk will take only around ten minutes. Nina sleeps soundly, and she knows how to wake up alone and wait for me calmly; that's how we do it at home, when I go down to buy something in the morning. For the first time I walk in the opposite direction from the lake, toward the green house. "Sooner or later something bad is going to happen," my mother would say. "And when it happens I want to have you close."

*Your mother is not important.*

I like to look at the houses and the grounds, the countryside. I think I could keep walking like that for hours.

*It's possible. I do it sometimes at night.*

And Carla lets you?

*It's a mistake to talk about me right now. How is the walk, in your body?*

I walk quickly; I like it when my breathing grows

rhythmic and my thoughts shrink to the essential. I think about the walk and nothing else.

*That's good.*

I remember the way Carla's hand moved in the car. "The people who live here take that way out," she'd said. Her arm reached to her right, and her hand held her cigarette at the height of my mouth, the cigarette sharpening the directions. Over there the houses have a lot more land. Some have sown fields that reach back half a hectare; a few have wheat or sunflowers, but really it's almost all soy. Crossing a few more lots, behind a long line of poplar trees, a narrower lane opens off to the right and goes along a small but deep stream.

*Yes.*

A few more modest houses stand along the stream bank, squeezed in between the fine, dark thread of water and the wire of the next estate. The next-to-last one is painted green. The color is worn but it's still bright, it stands out from the rest of the landscape. I stop for a second and a dog comes out of the field.

*This is important.*

Why? I need to understand which things are important and which aren't.

*What happens with the dog?*

He pants and wags his tail, and he's missing a back leg.

*Yes, this is very important, this has a lot to do with what we're looking for.*

He crosses the street, looks at me for a moment, and continues on toward the houses. There's no one in sight, and since strange things always seem like warnings to me, I turn around and head home.

*Something is going to happen now.*

Yes. When I reach the house I see Carla waiting in the doorway. She moves away from the house a few steps and looks up, maybe toward the bedroom windows. She's wearing a red cotton dress now, and the straps of the bikini peek out on her shoulders. She never goes into the house, she waits for me outside. Outside we chat and sunbathe, but if I go in to get more iced tea or put on sunscreen, she always waits outside.

*Yes.*

She sees me, she wants to say something to me and she seems not to know whether to walk toward me or not. She can't seem to decide what's best. Then I feel it with frightening clarity as the rope pulls taut: the shifting rescue distance.

*This clearly leads us right to the exact moment.*

Carla gestures, raising her hands as if she doesn't understand what is happening. And I have a terrifying feeling of doom.

"What? What's wrong?" I ask her, shouting.

"He's in your house. David is in your house."

"What do you mean, he's in my house?"

Carla points toward my daughter's room, on the second floor. The palm of a hand is pressed against the glass, and then Nina appears, smiling: she must be on a stool or her desk. She sees me and waves through the glass. She looks cheerful and calm, and for a moment I am grateful that my sense of dread isn't working right, that it was all a false alarm.

*But it wasn't.*

No. Nina says something that I can't hear, and she repeats it, using her hands as a megaphone, excited. Then I remember that when I left the house all the

windows had been open because of the heat, upstairs
and downstairs. Now they are all shut tight.

"Do you have a key?" asks Carla. "I couldn't open
either of the doors."

I walk toward the house, almost running, and
Carla runs behind me.

"We have to get in fast," says Carla.

This is insane, I think. David is just a little boy.
But I can't help it now, I'm running. I dig in my
pocket for the keys and I'm so nervous that even
though I have them between my fingers, I can't get
them out.

"Hurry, hurry," says Carla.

I have to get away from this woman, I tell myself
as I finally manage to get the keys out. I open the
door and let her in behind me; she follows me very
closely. This is terror itself, entering a house I still

barely know in search of my daughter, so afraid I can't even utter her name. I race up the stairs, and Carla follows me. Whatever is happening must be truly terrible to finally get your mother to come inside the house.

"Hurry, hurry," she says.

I have to get this woman out of my house right now. We go up the first flight of stairs in two or three steps, then the second. The hallway has two rooms to either side. There is no one in the first, the one Nina was waving from, and I stay there an instant longer than necessary because I have the idea they could be hiding. In the second room I don't see them either; I look in corners and unlikely places, as if, secretly, my mind were preparing to face something immense.

The third room is mine. Like the previous ones,

the door is closed, and I open it quickly, taking a few steps into the room. It's David. So this is David, I say to myself. I see you, for the first time.

*Yes.*

You're standing in the middle of the room, looking toward the door like you're waiting for us. Maybe even wondering what all the fuss is about.

"Where is Nina?" I ask you.

You don't answer.

*I don't know where Nina is right then, and I don't know you.*

"Where is Nina?" I repeat, shouting.

You aren't frightened or surprised at my excitement. You seem tired, bored. If it weren't for the white spots you have on your skin, you'd be a normal, everyday boy. That's what I thought.

"Mommy." It's Nina's voice.

I turn back toward the hallway. She is holding Carla's hand and she looks at me fearfully.

"What's wrong?" asks Nina, wrinkling her forehead, about to start crying.

"Are you okay? Are you okay, Nina?" I ask.

Nina hesitates, but maybe that's because she sees how furious I am, indignant with Carla and all of her madness.

"This is crazy," I tell your mother. "You're completely insane."

Nina pulls away from Carla.

You're all alone, I tell myself. You'd better get this woman out of the house as soon as possible.

"Things always end up like this with David." Carla's eyes fill with tears.

"David didn't do anything!" And now I'm really

shouting, now I'm the one who seems crazy. "You're the one scaring us with all your delusions of . . ."

I look at you. Your eyes are red, and the skin around your eyes and mouth is a little thinner than is normal, a little pinker.

"Get out." I say it to Carla, but I'm looking at you.

"Let's go, David."

Your mother doesn't wait for you. She walks away and goes downstairs. She walks upright, elegant in her red dress and gold bikini. I feel Nina's hand, small and soft, carefully take my own. You don't move.

"Go with your mother," I tell you.

You don't refuse or answer. You're just there, as though switched off. I'm annoyed that you don't move, but I'm more annoyed by Carla now, and I decide to go down and make sure she leaves the house.

I have to do it slowly, waiting for Nina, who doesn't want to let go of my hand. Now in the kitchen, before going out, Carla turns around to say something to me, but my look dissuades her and she leaves in silence. Is this the exact moment?

*No, this isn't the exact moment.*

It's hard when I don't know what I'm looking for.

*It's something in the body. But it's almost imperceptible, we have to pay attention.*

That's why the details are so important.

*Yes, that's why.*

But how could I let them get between us so quickly? How can it be that leaving Nina alone for a few minutes, sleeping, could mean so much danger and madness?

*This isn't the exact moment. Let's not waste time on this.*

Why do we have to go so quickly, David? Is there so little time left?

*Very little.*

Nina is still in the kitchen, looking at me disconcertedly, shaking off her fear by herself. I pull a chair over so she can sit down, and I start making a snack. I'm very nervous, but doing things with my hands frees me from giving her explanations, it gives me time to think.

"Is David going to eat too?" asks Nina.

I put the kettle on the stove and look upward. I think about your eyes, and I wonder if you're still standing in the middle of the room.

*Why? This is important.*

I don't know. Now that I think about it, you're not what scares me.

*What is?*

Do you know what it is, David?

*Yes, it has to do with the worms. We're getting closer and closer to the exact moment.*

I sit up in my chair, alert.

*Why? What's happening?*

I see you outside, in the yard, and I don't understand how you got there. I was watching the stairs the whole time. You go over to the sandals Carla left behind, you pick them up, walk to the edge of the pool, and throw them in. You look around and find Carla's towel and scarf, and you throw those into the water too. My sandals and glasses are nearby, you see them, but they don't seem to interest you. Now that you are in the sun, I see some spots on your body that I hadn't noticed before. They're subtle; one covers the right part of your forehead and almost your whole mouth, other spots cover your arms and one of your legs. You look like Carla, and I think that without the spots you would be a really lovely boy.

*What else?*

You seem to be leaving, and when you're finally gone I feel calmer. I open the windows, I sit down for a moment on the living room sofa. It's a strategic place because from there I can see the front gate, the yard, and the pool, and in the other direction I can keep my eye on the kitchen. Nina is still sitting and eating the last of the cookies; she seems to understand that it isn't a good time to take her cheerful laps around the house.

*And what else?*

I make a decision. I realize I don't want to be here anymore. The rescue distance is so short now I don't think I can be more than a few steps away from my daughter. The house, its grounds, the whole town seems like an unsafe place after today, and there's no reason to take any risks. I know that my next move will be to pack our bags and get out of here.

*What are you worried about?*

I don't want to spend another night in the house, but leaving right away would mean driving too many hours in the dark. I tell myself I'm just scared, that it's better to rest so tomorrow I can think about things more clearly. But it's a terrible night.

*Why?*

Because I don't sleep well. I wake up several times. Sometimes I think it's because the room is too big. The last time I wake up, it's still dark out. It's raining, but that's not what alarms me when I open my eyes. It's the violet light coming from Nina's bedside table. I call her name, but she doesn't answer. I get out of bed and put on my robe. Nina isn't in her room, or in the bathroom. I go downstairs clutching the railing; I'm still half asleep. The light in the kitchen is on. Nina is sitting at the table, her bare little feet dangling in the air. I wonder if she is sleep-walking, if this is what sleepwalking children do, and also if that's what you do at night, when Carla says she finds your bed empty and you're not in the house. But of course, that's not important now, right?

*No.*

I take a few more steps toward the kitchen and I see that my husband is there, sitting across the table from Nina. It's an impossible image—how could he have come in without my hearing him? He's not sup-posed to be here until the weekend. I lean against the doorway. Something's happening, something's hap-pening, I tell myself, but I'm still half asleep. He has his hands folded on the table, he's leaning toward

Nina and looking at her with his brow furrowed. Then he looks at me.

"Nina has something to tell you," he says.

But Nina looks at her father and copies the position of his hands on the table. She doesn't say anything.

"Nina . . ." says my husband.

"I'm not Nina," says Nina.

She leans back and crosses one leg over the other in a way I have never seen her do before.

"Tell your mother why you aren't Nina," says my husband.

"It's an experiment, Miss Amanda," she says, and she pushes a can toward me.

My husband takes the can and turns it so I can see the label. It's a can of peas of a brand I don't buy, one I would never buy. They're a bigger, much harder kind of pea than what we eat, coarser and cheaper. A product I would never choose to feed my family with, and that Nina can't have found in our cupboards. On the table, at that early-morning hour, the can has an alarming presence. This is important, right?

*This is very important.*

I go over to her.

"Where did this can come from, Nina?" My question sounds harsher than I would like.

And Nina says:

"I don't know who you're talking to, Miss Amanda."

I look at my husband.

"Who are we talking to?" he asks, playing along.

Nina opens her mouth, but no sound comes out. She keeps it open for a few seconds, wide open, as if she were screaming, or exactly the opposite, as if she needed a lot of air and couldn't get it. It's a terrifying gesture I've never seen her make before. My husband leans over the table toward her, then a little more. I think he simply can't believe it. When Nina finally closes her mouth, he suddenly sits down again, as if someone had been holding him up the whole time by an invisible lapel, and now they'd let go of him.

"I'm David," says Nina, and she smiles at me.

*Is this a joke? Are you making this up?*

No, David. It's a dream, a nightmare. I wake up agitated, this time completely clearheaded. It's five in the morning, and a few minutes later I'm already packing one of the three suitcases we arrived with. At six I have everything almost ready. You like these observations, David.

*They're necessary. They help with remembering.*

The thing is, I think over and over how strange my fear is, and it seems ridiculous to be already loading things into the car, with Nina still in her room, asleep.

*You're trying to get away.*

Yes. But in the end I don't, do I?

*No.*

Why not, David?

*That's what we're trying to find out.*

I go up to Nina's room. I pack her bag while I try to wake her up. I'd made her some tea, and I brought it up with her packet of cookies. She wakes up and has breakfast in bed, still sleepy, watching me fold the last articles of clothing, put away her markers, stack her books. She's so sleepy that she doesn't even insist on knowing where we are going, why we are going back sooner than planned.

My mother always said something bad would happen. My mother was sure that sooner or later something bad would happen, and now I can see it with total clarity, I can feel it coming toward us like a tangible fate, irreversible. Now there's almost no rescue distance, the rope is so short that I can barely move in the room, I can barely walk away from Nina to go to the closet and grab the last of our things.

"Get up," I tell her. "Come on, let's go."

Nina gets out of bed.

"Get your shoes. Put on this jacket."

I take her hand and we go down the stairs together. Upstairs, the violet light on Nina's bedside table is still on; downstairs, I see the light coming from the kitchen. It's all just like in the dream, I say to myself, but as long as I have Nina by the hand, her strangely stiff body won't be waiting for me in the kitchen, she won't talk to me in your voice, there will be no perplexing can of peas on the table.

*Good.*

By now there's a little light outside. Instead of putting Nina in the car right away, I have her pack things up with me so she doesn't leave my side. We also go around the house together to close the shutters.

*You're wasting time.*

Yes, I know.

*Why?*

I'm thinking. While I'm closing the shutters I'm thinking about Carla, about you, and I tell myself that I am part of this insanity.

*Yes.*

I mean, if I really wasn't letting myself be taken in by your mother's fears, none of this would be happening. I'd be getting up right now, putting on my bikini to make the most of the morning sun.

*Yes.*

So I'm guilty too, then. I'm confirming your mother's own madness for her. But that's not how it's going to be.

*No?*

No. That's why I have to tell her.

*You're thinking of talking to Carla.*

Of apologizing for yelling at her yesterday. I want to convince her everything is okay, and that she has to calm down.

*That's a mistake.*

If I don't do it, I can't leave in good conscience. I'll be back in the city and still be thinking about all this craziness.

*Talking to Carla is a mistake.*

I turn off the main power switch and close the front door of the house.

*This is the moment to leave town, now is the time.*

I leave the keys in the mailbox, just as Mr. Geser told me to do the day we leave.

*But you're going to see Carla.*

Is that why I don't make it?

*Yes, that's why.*

We leave at dawn. I go down the road in the opposite direction from town and then stop at your house. I'd never gone inside your house, and I'd really rather not. So what I find there comes as good news: the house is empty, and I remember it is Tuesday. Everything starts too early in the country, and maybe your mother is already at Sotomayor's offices, a mile toward town. It's a relief, and I take it as a sign that I'm doing the right thing. Nina is sitting behind me, looking out in silence as we drive away from your house toward Sotomayor's. She doesn't seem worried. She's wearing her seat belt, her legs crossed Indian style on the seat, as always, and she's hugging her mole. Sotomayor's fields start at a big manor house, and they open out behind it, indefinite. There is still no sidewalk, but there is grass between the street and the house. There are two medium-sized sheds behind it, and seven silos much farther back, far beyond the first fields. I leave the car next to others that are parked at the side of the house, on the grass. I ask Nina to get out with me. The door is open, and we enter the house holding hands. Just as Carla told me, the place is more office than house. There are two men drinking *mate*, and a fat young woman is signing papers and reading the titles of each page under her breath. One of the men nods, as if he were mentally following the woman's activity. Everything stops when they see us, and the woman asks us what we need.

"I'm looking for Carla."

"Ah." She looks at both of us again, as if the first time hadn't been enough. "Just a moment, she'll be right back."

"You two want some *mate*?" One of the men at the table raises the gourd, and I wonder if either of them is Sotomayor.

I shake my head and we walk toward a sofa, but then Carla is already back. No one lets her know we're here, and she's so distracted when she comes in that she doesn't notice us. She's wearing a white cotton shirt, and I'm almost startled not to see the gold bikini straps peeking out.

*We need to go faster.*

Why? What's going to happen when the time is up?

*I'll tell you when it's important to know the details.*

When she finally sees us, Carla is surprised. She thinks something is wrong, and she gets scared. She looks at Nina out of the corner of her eye. I tell her everything is fine. That I only want to apologize for yesterday, and to tell her I'm leaving.

"Where are you going?"

"We're going back," I say. "Back to the capital."

Her frown makes me feel sorry for her, or guilty, I don't know.

"My husband needs me there, we have to go back."

"Now?"

If we had gone without saying goodbye it would have been terrible for your mother, and in spite of the awkwardness I congratulate myself for having come to see her.

*But it's not a good idea.*

It's already done.

*This is not good at all.*

From one moment to the next your mother's hurt

expression completely changes. She wants us to see Omar's stables. They're abandoned, but they're contiguous to Sotomayor's land and it's easy to get there from here.

*The important thing is very close now. What else is happening? Around you, what's happening?*

It's true, something else is happening. It's outside, while your mother is trying to convince us to go with her. I hear a truck pull up and stop. The men drinking *mate* put on long plastic gloves and go out. There's another male voice coming from outside, maybe the truck driver's. Carla says she's going to drop off some papers and then she'll take us to the stables, and she tells us to wait outside. And then there's a noise. Something falls, something plastic and heavy, but it doesn't break. We leave Carla and go outside. There are two men unloading plastic drums. They are big, and the men struggle to carry one in each hand. There are a lot, the truck is full of barrels.

*This is it.*

One of the drums is left alone in the doorway to the shed.

*This is the important thing.*

This is the important thing?

*Yes.*

How can this be so important?

*What else?*

Nina sits down in the grass near the truck. She watches the men work, and she seems fascinated with their activity.

*What are the men doing, exactly?*

The driver is in the truck bed, and he's the one who hands the drums down. The other two take turns receiving them and carrying them inside. They go in a different door, the big door to a shed that's a little farther back. There are a lot of barrels; the men come and go, over and over. The sun is strong and there is a fresh, pleasant breeze. I think how this is our goodbye to the place, and that maybe this is Nina's way of saying goodbye. So I sit down next to her and we watch them work together.

*What else, in the meantime?*

I don't remember much else, that's all that is happening.

*No, there's more. Around you, close by. There's more.*

That's all.

*The rescue distance.*

I'm sitting ten inches away from my daughter, David. There is no rescue distance.

*There must be. Carla was only steps away from me the day the stallion escaped and I almost died.*

I have a lot of questions to ask you about that day.

*Now's not the time. You don't feel anything? There's no other sensation that could be tied to something else?*

Something else?

*What else is happening?*

Carla takes a while to come outside. We're very close to everything, in the middle of their work, almost in the way. But it all happens slowly and pleasantly, the men are nice and they smile at Nina again and again. When they finish unloading the drums, they wave the driver off and the truck drives away. The men go back into the house, and we get up from the grass. I look at my watch and it's a quarter to nine. Nina looks at her clothes. She turns to look at her bottom, her legs.

*Why? What's wrong?*

"What's wrong?" I ask her.

"I'm soaked," she says, somewhat indignantly.

"Let's see . . ." I take her hand and spin her around. With the color of her clothes I can't tell how wet she is, but I touch her and yes, she's wet.

"It's dew," I tell her. "It'll dry while we're walking."

*This is it. This is the moment.*

It can't be, David, this is really all there is.

*That's how it starts.*

My God.

*What is Nina doing?*

She's such a pretty girl.

*What is she doing?*

She walks away a little.

*Don't let her walk away.*

She looks at the grass. She touches it with her hands, like she can't believe her small disgrace.

*What's happening with the rescue distance?*

Everything is fine.

*No.*

She's frowning.

"Are you okay, Nina?" I ask her.

She smells her hands.

"It's really gross," she says.

Carla comes out of the house, finally.

*Carla isn't important.*

But I walk over to her. I think I'm still trying to dissuade her from the walk.

*Don't leave Nina alone. It's happening right now!*

Carla comes over, carrying her bag and smiling.

*Don't get distracted.*

I can't choose what happens next, David. I can't turn back toward Nina.

*It's happening.*

What is, David? My God, what is happening?

*The worms.*

No, please.

*It's a very bad thing.*

Yes, the rope pulls tight, but I'm distracted.

*What's on Nina?*

I don't know, David, I don't know! I'm talking to Carla like an idiot. I ask her how long it will take us to walk to the stables.

*No, no.*

I can't do anything, David. Is this how I lose her? The rope is so taut now I feel it in my stomach. What's happening?

*This is the most important thing. This is everything we need to know.*

Why?

*What is the feeling now, exactly now?*

I'm soaked too. I'm wet, yes, I feel it now.

*That's not what I mean.*

It's not important that I'm wet, too?

*It is important, but it's not what we need to under-stand. Amanda, this is the moment, don't get distracted. We're looking for the exact moment because we want to know how it starts.*

It's just, I'm focused on something else. Now I feel it, yes, I'm soaked.

*It's very gradual.*

The breeze cools the dampness and I feel the wet seat of my pants. Carla tells me it will take only about twenty minutes, the stables are just right over there, and I look instinctively at my pants.

*Nina looks at you.*

Yes.

*She knows this is not good.*

But it's dew. I still think it's dew.

*It's not dew.*

What is it, David?

*We've come this far so we can learn exactly what you feel right now.*

Just that slight tug in my stomach from the rope, and something acidic, just barely, under my tongue.

*Acidic, or bitter?*

Bitter, bitter, yes. But it's so subtle, my God, so subtle. We start to walk, the three of us, crossing the lot and going deeper into the fields. Nina gets distracted. Carla tells her there's a well at the stable, and now she's excited to get there too. Her mood changes.

*How long does that take?*

Right away, she forgets right away. So do I.

*Are you going to wonder again what it was that got you wet?*

No, David.

*Are you going to smell your hands?*

No.

*You're not going to do anything?*

No, David, I'm not going to do anything. We're going to walk and I'm even going to wonder if I'm doing the right thing by leaving. We talk, we stay there under the sun with the grass up to our knees. It's an almost perfect moment. Carla talks to me about Sotomayor. Your mother has made some decisions about how to arrange the order spreadsheets, and Sotomayor has been praising her all morning.

*Don't you realize what's happening right now?*

I can't realize, David. Nina sees the well and runs over to it. The stables don't have a roof, there are just some burned bricks. It's a beautiful view, but also desolate, and when I ask Carla how they burned, she just seems annoyed.

"I brought *mate*," she says.

I tell Nina to be careful. I'm surprised by how much I want to drink a few *mate*s, how little I feel like getting into the car and driving four and a half hours to the capital. Returning to the noise, the grime, the congestion of everything.

*Does this place really seem better to you?*

A group of trees gives us some shade, and we sit near the trunks, close to the well. The soy fields stretch out to either side of us. It's all very green, a perfumed green, and Nina asks me if we can't stay a little longer. Just a little.

*I'm not interested in this anymore.*

"A lot of things have happened," I say to Carla.

She wrinkles her brow while she takes out the *mate*, but she doesn't ask what I'm referring to.

"I mean, since you started telling me about David."

*Really, this won't get us anywhere. If you knew how valuable time was right now you wouldn't use it for this.*

I like this moment. We're good, all three of us at ease. After this everything starts to go bad.

*When does it start to go bad, exactly?*

"What happened with David? What was it that changed so much?" I ask Carla.

"The spots," says Carla, and she shrugs one of her shoulders, almost nonchalantly, like a little girl. "At first the spots were what bothered me most."

Nina walks around the well, and every few steps she stops and leans over the bricks toward the darkness. She says her name, she says "We adore it" in her noble tone of voice, and the echo of her voice is just a little deeper. She says "Hello," "Nina," "Hello, I am Nina and we adore this."

"But there were other things," says Carla, and she

hands me the *mate*. "You think I'm exaggerating, and that I'm the one who's driving the boy crazy. Yesterday, when you yelled at me after David went into your house . . ."

Where are her gold straps? I think. Carla is pretty. Your mother, she's very pretty, and there's something in the memory of those straps that moves me. I feel so bad for yelling at her.

"The spots appeared later. Because the first days, even though the woman in the green house said David would survive, his body was boiling and he was delirious with fever. It wasn't until the fifth day that it started to subside."

"What was it that poisoned him?"

Carla shrugged her shoulder again.

"It happens, Amanda. We're in the country, there are sown fields all around us. People come down with things all the time, and even if they survive they end up strange. You see them on the street. Once you learn to recognize them you'll be surprised how many there are." Carla hands me the *mate* so she can take out her cigarettes. "The fever passed, but it took a long time for David to start speaking again. Then, little by little, he started to say a few words. But really, Amanda, the way he talked was so strange."

"Strange in what way?"

"Strange can be quite normal. Strange can just be the phrase 'That is not important' as an answer for everything. But if your son never answered you that way before, then the fourth time you ask him why he's not eating, or if he's cold, or you send him to bed, and he answers, almost biting off the words as if he were still learning to talk, 'That is not important,' I swear to you, Amanda, your legs start to tremble."

And isn't this important, David? Aren't you going to say anything about this?

"Maybe it's something he heard the woman in the green house say," I tell her. "Maybe it's part of the shock from everything he went through when he had the fever."

"I thought something like that, too. Then one day, I was lying on my bed and I saw him in the backyard. He was kneeling down with his back to me, I couldn't really understand what he was doing, but it bothered me. I couldn't tell you why, but something in his movements alarmed me."

"I understand perfectly."

"Yes, it's an instinct that comes with being a mother. Anyway, I stopped what I was doing and went outside. I took a few steps toward him, but when I realized what was happening I stayed where I was, I couldn't take another step. He was burying a duck, Amanda."

"A duck?"

"He was four and a half years old, and he was burying a duck."

"Why was he burying a duck? Do they come from the lake?"

"Yes. I called to him but he ignored me. I knelt down, because he was looking down and I wanted to see his face, I wanted to understand what was happening, not just with the duck, but with him. His face was red, his eyes swollen from so much crying. He was digging up dirt with his plastic shovel. Its broken handle was lying on the ground to one side, and now he was digging with only the spoon part of the shovel, which was only slightly bigger than his hand. The duck lay to one side. Its eyes were open, and stretched out like that on the ground, its neck seemed longer and more flexible than normal. I tried to figure out what had happened, but at no point did David look up."

*I want to show you something.*

I'm the one who decides what to focus on in the story now, David. Doesn't what your mother is telling me strike you as important?

*No.*

Your mother is smoking, and Nina takes a few spirited laps around the well. This will now be the important thing.

"Really," says your mother, "if your son beats a duck to death, or strangles it, or kills it however he killed it—it doesn't have to be so terrible. Here in the country those things happen, and worse things probably go on in the capital. But a few days later I found out what happened, I saw it with my own eyes."

"Mommy," says Nina. "Mommy." But I don't pay attention. I'm focused on Carla, and Nina moves away again.

"I was sunbathing in the backyard. About a hundred feet away we have wheat growing. It's not ours, Omar rents the land out to the neighbors, and I like it because it makes our yard smaller, more intimate. David was sitting near my chair, playing on the ground with his things. Then he stood up, looking off toward the wheat field. I saw him with his back to me, small and strange with his arms hanging down by the sides of his body and his little fists clenched, as if he'd been startled by something threatening."

I feel something strange in my hands, David.

*In your hands? Now?*

Yes, now.

"David was motionless, his back to me, for about two minutes. That's a long time, Amanda. And that whole time I was thinking about calling out to him, but I was afraid to do it. Then something moved in among the wheat. And then a duck appeared. It was walking strangely. It took one or two steps toward us and it stopped."

"Like it was afraid?"

I heard Nina running around the well. I heard her say, "We adore it, we adore it, we adore it," her laughter and the echo of her laughter coming closer and moving away. Carla exhaled her cigarette smoke and kept thinking about my question.

"No. Like it was exhausted. They looked at each other, I swear they did. David and the duck looked at each other for a few seconds. And the duck took a few more steps, one foot crossing in front of the other like it was drunk, or had lost control of its body, and when it tried to take the next step it slumped to the ground, dead."

My hands are shaking now, David.

*They're shaking?*

I think so, yes. They're shaking, I don't know. Maybe it's Carla's story.

*Do you feel like they're shaking, or are they really shaking?*

I'm looking at my hands now and I can't see them shake. Does this have to do with the worms?

*It has to do with them, yes.*

I'm looking at my hands but your mother keeps talking. She says that the next morning, while she was washing the dishes, she saw that there were three more dead ducks in the yard, stretched out on the ground just like the day before.

*I want to know what else is happening with your hands.*

But is it true, David? Did you kill those ducks? And now your mother tells me that you buried them all, and that you cried each time.

"I saw it all from the window, Amanda, one hole beside the next and all that time I was standing with a half-washed saucepan in my hand. I didn't have the strength to go outside."

Is it true?

*I buried them. Burying isn't the same as killing.*

Carla says there's more, that there's something worse she wants to tell me.

*Amanda, I need you to pay attention, there's something I want to show you.*

She says it's about a dog, one of Mr. Geser's dogs.

*Each thing she tells you is going to be worse, but if you don't stop this story now we're not going to have enough time for what I have to show you.*

I'm confused. Right now I can only concentrate on Carla's story.

*Do you see me?*

Yes.

*Where am I?*

I'd forgotten, but yes, you're here, sitting on the edge of my bed. It's high, and your feet hang in the air. When you move, it makes the iron frame creak under the mattress. It's been making noise this whole time.

*Where are we?*

I know where we are. In the emergency clinic, we've been here awhile now.

*Do you know for how long?*

A day, or five.

*Two.*

And Nina? Where is Nina right now? The men unloading the barrels smile when they pass us, they're nice to her, but now she gets up from the grass and shows me her dress, her hands. Her hands are wet, but it's not from dew, is it?

*No. Can you get up?*

Get out of bed?

*I'm going to get down.*

The bed is creaky.

*Do you see me?*

What makes you think I can't see?

*Put your feet on the floor.*

Why are you in pajamas?

*If you take twelve steps forward we'll reach the hallway.*

Where is Nina? Does my husband know I'm here?

*If you need, I can turn the lights on.*

Your mother tells me that the dog made it to the stairs of your house, and sat there for almost a whole afternoon. She says she asked you about the dog several times, and each time you replied that the dog wasn't the important thing. She says you locked yourself in your room and refused to come out. She says that only when the dog finally slumped to the ground the way she'd seen the ducks do, only then did you come out of the house. You dragged the dog to the backyard, and you buried it.

*If you need to, you can lean on my shoulder.*

Why is Carla so afraid of you?

*Do you see the drawings on the walls?*

They're children's drawings. Nina draws, too.

*How old are these children? Could you say how old they are?*

David.

*Yes.*

I'm confused, I'm mixing up times.

*You told me.*

Yes, but I understand clearly what is happening, at certain moments.

*I think that's true.*

What are you going to show me? I don't know if I want to see it.

*Careful with the stairs.*

Slower, please.

*There are six steps and then the hallway continues.*

Where are we?

*These are the rooms in the emergency clinic.*

It seems like a big place.

*Everything is small here. It's just that we're walking slowly. Do you see the drawings?*

Are there drawings of yours?

*At the end of the hall.*

Is the clinic a day-care center too?

*Here I am with the ducks, the dog, and the horses, this is my drawing.*

What horses?

*Carla will tell you about the horses.*

What are you going to show me?

*We're almost there.*

Your mother has a gold bikini, and when she moves in the driver's seat the perfume from her sunscreen wafts through the car. Now I realize: she makes that movement on purpose, she intentionally lets the strap fall.

*Do you still see me? Amanda, I need you to focus. I don't want to start again from the beginning.*

From the beginning? Have we already done this other times? Where is Nina?

*We're going to go through this door. Here.*

Is this happening because of the worms?

*Yes, in a way. I'm going to turn on the light.*

What is this place?

*A classroom.*

It's a preschool. Nina would like this place.

*It's not a preschool. I call it the waiting room.*

I don't feel good, this isn't a waiting room, David.

*What do you feel right now?*

I think I have a fever. Is that why everything is so confused? I think that's why, and also because your attitude is not helpful.

*I'm trying to be as clear as possible, Amanda.*

That's not true. I'm missing the most important information.

*Nina.*

Where is Nina? What happens at the exact moment? Why is all this about worms?

*No, no. It's not about worms. It feels like worms, at first, in your body. But Amanda, we've been through all this, too. We've already talked about the poison, the contamination. You've already told me four times how you got here.*

That's not true.

*It is true.*

But I don't know, I still don't know.

*You know. But you don't understand.*

I'm about to die.

*Yes.*

Why? My hands are shaking a lot.

*I don't see them shaking.*

Back in the field, they're shaking now as I watch Nina leave the well and come over to me.

*Amanda, I need you to concentrate.*

Carla asks me if I understand now, if in her place I wouldn't have felt the same way. And now Nina is very close by.

*Amanda, don't get distracted.*

She's frowning.

*Do you still see me?*

"What's wrong, Nina? Are you okay?"

Nina looks at her hands.

"It stings," she says. "My hands are burning."

"Then one day Omar wakes me up by shaking my feet," says Carla. "He's sitting on the bed, pale and rigid. I ask him what's wrong but he doesn't answer. It must be five, six in the morning, because there's hardly any light. 'Omar,' I say, 'Omar, what's wrong?' 'The horses,' he says. I swear to you, Amanda, the way he said it was terrifying. Every once in a while Omar could say some harsh things, but they never sounded the way those two words did. Sometimes he says ugly things about David. How he doesn't seem like a normal boy. That having David in the house makes him uncomfortable. He never wants to sit at the table with him. He hardly talks to him at all. Sometimes, we used to wake up at night and David wasn't in his room or anywhere else in the house, and that drove Omar crazy. I think it scared him. We never slept well, because we were intent on any sound. The first few times it happened, we went out looking for him. Omar went ahead with the flashlight and I held on to his shirt from behind. I focused on listening for any noises and on always staying close to him. One time before we left, Omar got a knife out and brought it with us, and I didn't say anything, Amanda. What can I tell you, it can get very dark in the country. Later, Omar started locking David in his room. He shuts him in before we go to bed and unlocks the door in the morning, before he leaves. There were times when David would bang on the door. He never calls for Omar. He pounds on the door and says my name—he doesn't call me Mom anymore, only Carla. So that day, Omar was sitting on the edge of the bed, and when I managed to wake up and realize something strange was happening, I leaned toward the door to see what he was staring at. The door to David's room was open. 'The horses,' said Omar. 'What's wrong with the horses?' I asked."

"They're stinging a lot, Mommy." Nina shows me her hands, sits down next to me. She hugs me.

I take her hands and plant a kiss on each one. She turns her palms up, to show me. Carla takes out a bag of little cookies and puts a handful into Nina's palms.

"This will cure anything," she says.

And Nina happily closes her hands and runs off toward the well, shouting her own name.

"And the horses?" I ask.

"They weren't there," says Carla.

"What do you mean they weren't there?"

"I asked Omar the same thing, and he said he'd heard a noise in the shed, that's what had woken him up. He saw David's door was open though he clearly remembered having locked it, and he got up to see what was happening. The front door was open too, and outside there was already a little light. He went out just like that, Omar told me, no flashlight and no knife. He looked at the fields, took a few steps away from the house, and for a second he didn't realize what it was that seemed so strange to him. He was half asleep. The horses weren't there. None of the horses. There was only a little foal, one that had been born four months before. It was standing alone in the middle of the pasture, and Omar says that already then, from the house, he was certain that the animal was frozen in fear. He approached it slowly. The foal didn't move. Omar looked to either side, looked toward the stream, toward the street, there was neither hide nor hair of the horses. He put the palm of his hand on the foal's forehead, he talked to it and nudged it a little, just to test the waters. But the foal didn't move. It stayed there until morning, when the police inspector and his two assistants came, and it was still there when they left. I saw it from the window. I swear to you, Amanda, I couldn't get up the courage to go out. But are you okay?"

"Yes, why?"

"You're pale."

"Did Omar know about the ducks? About Mr. Geser's dog?"

"He knew something. I'd decided not to tell him anything, but he saw the mounds of earth from the buried ducks, and he asked. When all that happened with the woman in the green house and the days of fever, he never asked questions. I think Omar suspected something and preferred not to know. Who knows, maybe he just wasn't interested. He was more concerned about the loss of his precious borrowed stallion. But you're pale, Amanda, your lips are white."

"I'm fine. Maybe something's not sitting right with me. I've been a little nervous," I say, thinking about yesterday's argument, and Carla looks at me out of the corner of her eye but doesn't say anything.

We sit in silence a moment. I want to ask about the

horses, but Carla is watching Nina now and I tell my-self it's better to wait. Nina is going back from the trees to the well. She's holding up the apron of her dress and using it as a basket, and when she gets to the well she kneels down with her dramatic affecta-tions of a princess, and she starts lining up pinecones on the ground.

"I really like her," says Carla. "Nina."

I smile, but I can sense there is something more behind her words.

"If I'd been able to choose, I would have wanted a girl. A girl like Nina."

Nearby, the breeze moving through the soy makes a soft, effervescent sound, as if caressing it, and the now bright sun comes and goes between the clouds.

"Sometimes I fantasize about leaving," says Carla. "About starting another life where I could have a

Nina of my own, someone I could take care of and who'd let me."

I want to talk to Carla, there are certain things I want to tell her, but my body is still and numb. And I'm like that for some seconds more, knowing that this is the moment to talk but immobile in the languid silence.

"Carla," I say.

The soy leans toward us now. I imagine how in just a few minutes I will leave the rented house behind, and Carla's house, I'll leave this town and year after year I will choose another kind of vacation, holidays at the beach and far from this memory. And she would come with me, that's what I believe: Carla would come if I suggested it, with nothing but her folders and the clothes on her back. Near my house we'd buy another gold bikini; I wonder if that would be the thing she'd miss the most.

*Do you see me? Can you see me now?*

Yes. But I'm on the floor, and it's hard to follow the story.

*Don't get up, better to stay on the floor a little longer.*

I think I lie down in the field, too.

*Carla helps you lie down.*

Yes, I see the treetops now.

*Because she asks you over and over if you're okay, but you don't answer. She puts her bag under your head, and she asks you what you had for breakfast, if you have low blood pressure, if you can hear her.*

How do you know that's what happens? Do you see it, were you hiding there?

*That's not the important thing now.*

Or is it because of what you said before, that we've already talked about the poisoning, that I already told you other times how I got here?

*Amanda.*

And Nina?

*Nina looks at the two of you from the well. She's left the pinecones scattered around her, and now there's nothing left of her royal airs.*

It's true, there's nothing left of her royal airs.

*Carla waits, but you don't say anything.*

But I'm awake.

*Yes, but you're not well.*

My hands are shaking, I told you.

*Nina runs toward you. Carla jumps up and heads her off. She distracts her a moment. She tells her you fell asleep and it's better to let you rest. She asks Nina to show her the well.*

Nina doesn't trust her.

*No, she doesn't trust her.*

I feel the rescue distance shorten, and it's because Nina doesn't trust Carla.

*But you can't do anything.*

I can't, no.

*If Carla goes to get help she'll have to leave you alone, or with Nina. I'm sure that's what Carla is thinking about now, and she doesn't know what to do.*

I'm so tired, David.

*This is a good moment for us.*

I fall asleep. Carla realizes it, and she leaves me alone for a bit while she plays with Nina.

*That's why it's a good moment. Do you see them?*

What?

*The names, on the waiting room wall.*

Are they the children who come to this room?

*Some of them aren't children anymore.*

But they all have the same handwriting.

*It's the writing of one of the nurses. The people whose names these are, they can't write, almost none of them can.*

They don't know how?

*Some of them do, they learned how to write, but they can't control their arms anymore, or they can't control their own heads, or they have such thin skin that if they squeeze the markers too much their fingers end up bleeding.*

I'm tired, David.

*What are you doing? It's not a good idea for you to get up now. Not yet. Where are you going? Amanda. That door doesn't open from inside, none of our doors can be opened from inside.*

I need you to stop. I'm exhausted.

*If you focus, things happen faster.*

Then they'll also end faster.

*Dying isn't so bad.*

And Nina?

*That's what we want to know now, isn't it? Sit down. Please, Amanda, sit down.*

My body hurts a lot, on the inside.

*That's the fever.*

It's not the fever, we both know it's not the fever. Help me, David. What's happening now at the stables?

*Carla and Nina play for a while around the well.*

Sometimes I open my eyes and see them. Carla hugs her constantly, and the rescue distance keeps tightening in my stomach, it wakes me up again and again. What's happening, David? Tell me what's happening in my body, please tell me.

*I tell you over and over, Amanda, but it's hard if you always ask again.*

It's as if I were dreaming.

*Some time goes by, and at a certain point you gather your strength and sit up. They both look at you, surprised.*

Yes.

*They come over to you, and Carla caresses your forehead.*

She has a very sweet perfume.

*Nina looks at you without coming too close, maybe she's starting to realize you aren't well. Carla says she'll go get the car, she laughs to alleviate the situation, she tells herself out loud that this is all so she will finally have the courage to drive alone, and so you will finally come over to her house for a cool drink. She's going to give you a cold iced tea with lemon and ginger, and that will cure everything.*

That won't cure anything.

*No, it won't cure anything. But you're feeling a little better, the discomfort comes and goes, that's how it always is at first. Carla tells Nina that she's leaving her in charge while she goes to get the car. She explains to Nina that she'll come back from the other direction, on the dirt road.*

Nina comes over to me, sits down, and hugs me.

*It takes Carla a while to come back.*

But Nina is so close that I don't care, and we stay like that for a long time. She's lying down, close against my body. She makes her hands into circles and brings them to her eyes, like binoculars.

"We like the treetops very much," she says.

*But you are thinking of the night.*

Our first night in the house, yes. Because hugging Nina reminds me of my first fears. I wonder if there could have been a warning in them. I walked, and the flashlight drew an oval in front of my feet. If I shone it forward to see what lay a little ahead of me, it was hard to see where I was stepping. The sound of the trees, the cars on the road every once in a while, and the barking of a dog confirmed that the country spread out immensely to either side, and that everything was miles away. And even so, blinded by the oval of light, as I walked I had the feeling I was moving deeper into a cave. I hunched over, and I moved forward taking short steps.

*And Nina?*

This is all about Nina.

*Where is Nina, during that first walk?*

She's sleeping in the house, soundly. But I can't sleep, not the first night. Before all else, I have to know what is around the house. Whether there are dogs, and if they're friendly, whether there are ditches, and how deep they are. Whether there are poisonous insects, snakes. I need to get out in front of anything that could happen, but everything is very dark and my eyes never get used to the darkness. I think I once had a very different idea of the night.

*Why do mothers do that?*

What?

*Try to get out in front of anything that could happen— the rescue distance.*

It's because sooner or later something terrible will happen. My grandmother used to tell my mother that, all through her childhood, and my mother would tell me, throughout mine. And now I have to take care of Nina.

*But you always miss the important thing.*

And what is the important thing, David?

*Nina sits up, she searches the horizon with her finger binoculars. Your own car drives up from the other side of the stables.*

For a moment I think it's my husband, I think he'll

get out and give us each a hug, and I'll be able to sleep peacefully the whole drive home, until I get to my bed in the city.

*But it's Carla. She gets out and walks toward you and Nina.*

She's barefoot and in her gold bikini. She skirts the pool and walks over the grass a little apprehensively, as if she weren't used to it or she remembered its texture with a little distrust. She forgets her sandals on the pool steps.

*No, Amanda, that was before. Now Carla skirts the stables.*

Because I'm on the ground, in the field.

*Exactly.*

But I always remember Carla with bare feet.

*She gets out of the car and leaves the door open. She approaches quickly, waiting for Nina to give her some sign about how things are going, but now Nina is sitting at your feet with her back to Carla, and she doesn't take her eyes off you. Carla helps you stand up, says you're already looking better. She loads everything into the car and takes Nina by the hand. She turns around to be sure you're following her, she tells you jokes.*

Carla.

*Yes, Carla.*

It's true, I do feel better. And the three of us are in the car again, like in the beginning, with your mother in the driver's seat. The car's engine stalls a few times, but your mother finally manages to put it in reverse. My mother said that the country is the best place to learn to drive. I learned in the country, when I was younger.

*That's not important.*

Yes, I figured.

*Carla doesn't feel very comfortable driving.*

But she does it well. Although we don't go in the direction I had expected.

"Where are we going, Carla?"

Nina is sitting in the backseat. She's pale, I realize now, and sweating. I ask her if she feels all right. Her legs are crossed Indian style, same as always, and as always she has her seat belt on, even though I haven't told her to buckle it. She makes an effort to lean toward us. She nods strangely, very slowly, and the rescue distance is so short that her body seems to pull on mine when she falls back into her seat. Carla straightens up again and again, but she can't relax. She looks at me from the corner of her eye.

"Carla."

"We're going to the clinic, Amanda. Let's see if we get lucky and someone can take a look at you."

*At the clinic they tell you everything is fine, and half an hour later you are all on the way home again.*

But why skip over it like that? We were following this story step by step. You're jumping ahead.

*None of this is important, and we're almost out of time.*

I need to see it all again.

*The important thing already happened. What follows are only consequences.*

Why does the story keep going, then?

*Because you still haven't realized. You still need to understand.*

I want to see what happens at the clinic.

*Don't drop your head like that, it makes it harder to breathe.*

I want to see what's happening now.

*I'm going to bring you a chair.*

No, we have to go back. We're still in the car on the

way to the emergency room. It's very hot and the sounds gradually grow more muffled. I almost can't hear the motor, and I'm surprised at how smoothly and silently the car moves over the gravel. A wave of nausea forces me to lean forward a moment, but it passes. My clothes are stuck to my body with sweat, and the sun's sharp reflection on the hood of the car makes me squint my eyes. Carla isn't in the driver's seat anymore. When I don't see her I feel disconcerted, frightened. She opens my door and her hands take hold of me, pull me out. The car doors close without making a sound, as if it weren't really happening, and still I see everything up close. I wonder if Nina is following us, but I can't turn to check or ask the question out loud. I see my feet walking and I wonder if I am the one moving them. We walk down this very hallway, the one behind me, outside the classroom.

*Lean your head here.*

Nina says something about the drawings, and hearing her voice calms me. She's still with us. The nape of Carla's neck moves a few steps ahead of me. I can stand up on my own, I tell myself, and the image of my hands against the wall, on the drawings, brings the intense burning back to my skin. Carla's hair is pulled back in a bun and the edge of the neck of her white shirt is stained a light green. It's from the grass, right? Another woman's voice tells us to come in and there she is, I feel Nina's hand in mine. I hold on tight and now she is the one who leads me. It's such a small hand, but I trust her. I tell myself that she will instinctively know what to do. I enter a small room and sit down on the cot. Nina asks what we're doing here, and I realize she has been asking what's going on the whole way here. What I need is to hug her again, but I can't even answer her. It's hard for me to say what I need to say. The woman, who is a nurse, checks my blood pressure, takes my temperature, looks at my throat and my pupils. She asks if my head hurts and I think yes, a lot, but Carla is the one who says it aloud.

"I have a terrible headache," I confirm, and the three of them sit there looking at me.

It's a shooting, intense pain that goes from the nape of my neck to my temples. I feel it now that it's been said out loud, and I can't feel anything else.

*How many hours have passed?*

Since when?

*Since what happened in front of Sotomayor's office.*

It's been about two hours since we left the office. Where were you, David?

*I was here, waiting for you.*

You were in the doctor's office?

*How do you feel now?*

Better, I feel better. It's such a relief to be somewhere without so much light.

*But we still have a few hours to go, we need to move forward. Is there something important about this moment?*

When I say I have a headache, Nina says she does too. And when I say I'm dizzy, Nina says she is too. The nurse leaves us alone for a moment, and your mother says to herself that she did the right thing in bringing us here. If your mother were five years older, she could be both of our mothers. Nina and I could have the same mother. A beautiful but tired mother who sits down now, and sighs.

"Carla, where is David?" I ask her.

But she isn't startled, she doesn't even look at me, and it's difficult to know if I'm really saying what I think I am, or if the questions are only in my head, mute.

Your mother takes her hair down from the bun and uses her hands like two big brushes, her slender fingers open and spread.

"Why aren't you with him, Carla?"

She shakes out her hair in a distracted movement. I'm sitting on the cot and Nina is sitting next to me. I don't know when she climbed up but she seems to have been here for a while. My hands are at either side of my legs, holding on to the edge of the cot because at times I think I might fall off. Nina is in the same position, but she's resting one of her hands on mine. She looks silently at the floor. I wonder if she is disoriented too. The nurse comes back humming a song, and still humming intermittently she opens some drawers and talks with Carla, who is putting her hair back up in its bun. The nurse wants to know where we are from, and when Carla tells her we're not from the town, that we're here on vacation, the nurse stops humming and stares at us, as if with this information she had to start the examination all over again. She's wearing a necklace with three gold figures: two girls and a boy, the three of them close together, almost on top of each other, squeezed between her enormous breasts.

*One of that woman's children comes to this waiting room every day.*

"No need to worry," she says. She opens up the same drawers again and takes out a blister pack of pills. "You've just had a little too much sun. The important thing is to rest: go home, take it easy, and don't be scared."

There's a water fountain just behind her, and she

fills two cups of water and hands one to each of us, and she also gives us each a pill. I wonder what they are having Nina take, if it's the same thing they give me.

"Carla," I say, and she turns toward me in surprise. "We have to call my husband."

"Yes," she says. "Nina and I were already talking about that," and her condescending tone bothers me, and it bothers me that she doesn't stand up right away to do the thing that I have finally managed to ask her to do.

"You each take one of these pills every six hours, be sure not to go back out in the sun, and lie down and take a little nap in a dark room," says the nurse, and she gives the blister pack to Carla.

On top of my hand, Nina's hand still seems to want to restrain me. It's a pale and dirty hand. The dew has dried and the lines of mud cross her skin from one side to the other. It's not dew, I know, but you don't correct me anymore. I'm so sad, David. David. It scares me when you don't say anything for so long. Every time you could say something but don't, I wonder if maybe I'm just talking to myself.

*It takes you a while to get back to the car. Carla leads you both by the hand, one on either side. You or Nina stop every few steps, and then the whole group waits. Then, in the car, the gravel keeps Carla gripping the steering wheel in silence. None of the three of you says anything when you drive past the door of the house you left that morning and Mr. Geser's dogs race across the yard and under the privet hedges to run alongside the car, barking. They are furious, but neither you nor Carla seems to notice them. The sun is already directly overhead, and you can feel the heat rising up from the floor. But nothing important happens, and nothing important is going to happen from here on. And I'm starting to think you're not going to understand, that going forward with this story doesn't make any sense.*

But things keep happening. Carla parks beside the three poplar trees at her house, and there are many more details you'll want to hear.

*It's not worth it anymore.*

Yes, it is worth it. Carla pushes the button on her seat belt and it whips back into place, and with that whipping noise, my perception of reality comes back clearly. Nina is sleeping in the backseat. She is pale, and even when I say her name a few times she doesn't wake up. Now that her dress is completely dry I see the haloes of discolored fabric, huge and amorphous, like a big school of jellyfish.

*Really, Amanda, there's no point.*

I have an intuition, I have to go on.

"I'm going to carry this precious little thing inside," says your mother, opening the door to the backseat, putting Nina's arm over her own shoulder and lifting her out of the car. "And you two are going to take a good nap."

I have to get out of here, I think. That is all I'm thinking while I see her struggle to close the car door with her foot, and then walk toward her house carrying my daughter. The rescue distance shortens and the rope that connects us pulls me to my feet, too. I follow them without taking my eyes from Nina's little arm hanging over Carla's back. There is no grass around Carla's house, it's all earth and dust. There's the entrance to the house in front and a small shed to one side. In the backyard, I can see the fences that must have been for the horses, but there are no animals in sight. I look for you. I'm worried about the possibility of finding you in the house. I want to take Nina and get back into the car. I don't want to go inside. But I need so badly to sit down, I need so badly to get out of the sun, to drink something cool, and my body goes inside after Nina's.

*This is not important.*

I know, David, but you're still going to listen to it all. It takes a minute for my eyes to get used to the darkness in the house. There isn't much furniture but there are a lot of random things. Such ugly and useless things, little angel ornaments, large plastic boxes piled up, gold and silver plates nailed to the wall, plastic flowers in giant ceramic vases. I had imagined a different house for your mother. Now Carla sits Nina down on the sofa. It's a wicker sofa with cushions. Across the room in the oval mirror I see myself, flushed and sweaty, and behind me I see

the plastic-strip curtain over the front door, and beyond, the poplar trees and the car. Carla says she's
going to make the iced tea. The kitchen opens up to
the left; I see her take an ice cube tray from the
freezer.

"I would have straightened up some if I'd known
you were coming," she says, reaching for two cups on
a shelf.

I take two steps toward the kitchen and I'm almost
next to Carla. Everything is small and dark.

"And I would have baked something. I told you
about the butter cookies I make, remember?"

I do remember. She talked about them the first day
we met. Nina and I had arrived that morning, and
my husband wouldn't be there until Saturday. I was
checking the mailbox because Mr. Geser had told us
he would leave a second set of keys there, just in case,

when I saw your mother for the first time. She was coming from her house carrying two empty plastic buckets, and she asked me if I'd noticed the way the water smelled too. I hesitated, because we had drunk a little as soon as we'd arrived, yes, but everything was new and if it smelled different it was impossible for us to know if that was a problem or how it always was. Carla nodded worriedly and went along the path that edged the lot our house was on. When she came back I was already settling our things in the kitchen. Through the window I saw her put down the buckets to open the gate, and then put them down again to close it. She was tall and thin, and though she was carrying a bucket on either side, now apparently full, she was upright and elegant as she walked. Her gold sandals traced a whimsically straight line, as if she were practicing some kind of step or movement, and only when she reached the veranda did she raise her eyes and look at us. She wanted to leave me one of the buckets. She said it was better not to use the tap water that day. She insisted so much that I ended up accepting, and for a moment I wondered whether I should pay her for the water. Out of fear of offending her I offered, instead, to make some iced tea with lemon for the three of us. We drank it outside, with our feet in the pool.

"I make some mean butter cookies," said Carla. "They'd go perfectly with this iced tea."

"Nina would love those," I said.

"Indeed, we would adore them," said Nina.

In the kitchen at your house I fall into the chair beside the window. Your mother adds lemon to the tea and hands it to me with the sugar.

"Put a lot in," says Carla. "It'll clear your head."

And when Carla sees that I'm not touching the sugar, she sits in the other chair and stirs it in for me. She looks at me out of the corner of her eye.

I wonder if I'll be capable of getting myself out to the car. Then I see the graves. I just look outside, and there they are.

*There are twenty-eight graves.*

Twenty-eight graves, yes. And Carla knows I'm looking at them. She pushes my tea toward me. I don't see it but its cold nearness fills me with disgust. I won't be able to, I think. I feel bad about it for your mother's sake, but it's going to be impossible to drink anything. And yet I'm very thirsty. Carla waits. She stirs her tea and we are silent for a while.

"I miss him so much," she finally says, and I struggle to understand what she is talking about. "I checked all the kids his age, Amanda. All of them." I let her talk and I count the graves again. "I follow them without their parents' knowing. I talk to them, take them by the shoulders to look them right in the eyes."

*We have to move forward. We're losing time.*

Now your mother looks toward the backyard too.

"And there are so many graves, Amanda. When I hang up the clothes to dry I always look down at the ground, because I tell you, if I step on one of those mounds . . ."

"I need to go to the sofa," I say.

Your mother gets right up and goes with me. With one final effort I fall onto the sofa.

*I'm going to count to three, then let's get you up.*

Carla settles me in.

*One.*

She gives me a pillow.

*Two.*

I reach out my arm, and before I fall completely asleep, I hug Nina tightly against my body.

*Three. Grab the chair, like that. Sit down. Do you see me? Amanda?*

Yes. I see you. I'm very tired, David. And I have some terrifying nightmares.

*What do you see?*

Not here. Here I see you. Your eyes are very red, David, and you have almost no eyelashes left.

*In the nightmares.*

I see your father.

*That's because he's in the house. It's nighttime and my parents are looking at you and Nina lying on the sofa, and they're arguing.*

Your mother is going through my purse.

*She's not doing anything wrong.*

Yes, I know. I think she's looking for something. I

wonder if she's finally going to call my husband. That's all she has to do. Did I tell her enough times?

*You told her at the beginning, and now she's trying to find a phone number.*

Your father sits across from the sofa and looks at us. He looks at my untouched tea still on the table, he looks at my shoes, which your mother took off for me and left to one side of the sofa, and he looks at Nina's hands. You look a lot like your father.

*Yes.*

He has wide eyes, and though he would prefer we weren't there, he doesn't seem frightened. I sleep for moments at a time, and now the lights are off and everything is dark, it's night and your parents don't seem to be in the house. I think I see you. Do I see you? You're next to the plastic curtain but there's no light anymore, I can't see the poplars or the fields.

Now your mother walks past me and opens the window that looks out on the backyard. For a moment the air smells of lavender. I hear your father's voice. Now there's someone else. It's the woman from the emergency room. She's in the house, and your mother comes over with a glass of water. She asks me how I feel. I make an effort to sit up, and I swallow another pill from the blister pack. They also give one to Nina, who seems to be a little better and asks me something I can't answer.

*The effect comes and goes. You're poisoned.*

Yes. So why are they giving us something for sunstroke?

*Because the nurse is a very stupid woman.*

Then I go back to sleep.

*For several hours.*

Yes. But the nurse's son, the children who come to

this room, aren't they kids who've been poisoned? How can a mother not realize?

*Not all of them go through poisoning episodes. Some of them were born already poisoned, from something their mothers breathed in the air, or ate or touched.*

I wake up in the early morning.

*Nina wakes you up.*

"Can we go, Mommy?" she says while she's shaking me.

And I am so grateful to her. Her words are like a command, and it's as if she's just saved both our lives. I bring a finger to my lips to tell her we have to be quiet.

*You both feel a little better now, but it's an effect that comes and goes.*

I'm still dizzy, and I have to make a few attempts before I manage to stand up. My eyes are burning and

I rub them a couple times. I don't know how Nina feels. She ties her own shoes, though she still doesn't really know how to do it well. She is pale, but she doesn't cry or say anything. I'm standing now. I hold myself up by leaning against the wall, the oval mirror, the column in the kitchen. The car keys are next to my purse. I pick everything up slowly, careful not to make any noise. I feel Nina's hand on my leg. The door is open, and we hunch over as we go through the plastic curtain across the door. It's as if we were emerging from a cold, deep cave into the light. Nina lets go of me as soon as we leave the house. The car is unlocked, and we both get in through the driver's-side door. I close it, start the engine, and drive a few meters in reverse until I reach the gravel road. Before turning, in the rearview mirror, I look at your mother's house for the last time. For a moment I imagine her coming out in a bathrobe, making some kind of sign to me from the door of the house. But nothing moves. Nina climbs without any help into the back-seat and then buckles her seat belt.

"I need water, Mommy," she says, and crosses her legs on the seat.

And I think yes, of course, that's all we need now. It's been many hours and we haven't had a thing to drink, and poisoning is cured by drinking a lot of water. We're going to buy some bottles in town, I think. I'm thirsty too. The pills for sunstroke were on the kitchen table and I wonder if it wouldn't have been good to take another dose before getting out on the road. Nina is looking at me, her forehead wrinkled in a frown.

"Are you okay, Nina? Sweetie?"

Her eyes fill with tears but I don't ask again. We

are very strong, Nina and I, that's what I tell myself as I leave the gravel behind and the car finally bites the town's asphalt. I don't know what time it is, but there is still no one in the street. Where do you buy water in a town where everyone is asleep? I rub my eyes.

*Because you don't see well.*

It's like I need to rinse them out. There's a lot of light for it to be so early.

*But there isn't a lot of light. It's your eyes.*

There's something that's bothering my eyes. The shine from the asphalt and the pipes along the boulevard. I lower the visor and look for my sunglasses in the glove compartment. Every movement requires a huge effort. The light makes me squint, and it's hard to drive in these conditions. And my body, David. My body stings, a lot. Is it the worms?

*It feels like worms, minuscule worms all over your body. In a few minutes, Nina will be left alone in the car.*

No, David. That can't happen, what's Nina going to do alone in the car? No, please. This is it, isn't it? It's now. This is the last time I see Nina. There's something up ahead in the street, just before the corner. I'm going more slowly now, and I squint my eyes more. It's hard, David. It hurts a lot.

*Is it us?*

Who?

*The people crossing the street.*

It's a group of people. I see them and I put the brakes on, they're passing just inches away from the car. What are so many people doing together at this hour? They're children, almost all of them are children. What are they all doing crossing the street together, at that hour?

*They're taking us to the waiting room. That's where they leave us before the day starts. If we have a bad day they take us home early, but in general we don't go home until night.*

A woman stands at each corner to be sure the crosswalk is safe.

*It's difficult to care for us at home. Some parents don't even know how.*

The women wear the same apron as the woman from the emergency room.

*They're the nurses.*

There are children of all ages. It's very hard to see. I hunch down over the steering wheel. Are there healthy children too, in the town?

*There are some, yes.*

Do they go to school?

*Yes. But around here there aren't many children who are born right.*

"Mommy?" asks Nina.

*There are no doctors, and the woman in the green house does what she can.*

My eyes are watering, and I press them with both hands.

"Mommy, it's the girl with the giant head."

I open my eyes for a second and look forward. The girl from House & Home is standing stock-still in front of our car, looking at us.

*But I push her.*

Yes, it's true, you're the one who pushes her.

*She always needs a push.*

There are a lot of children.

*There are thirty-three of us, but the number changes.*

They are strange children. They're, I don't know,
my eyes are burning. Deformed children. They don't
have eyelashes, or eyebrows. Their skin is pink, very
pink, and scaly too. Only a few are like you.

*How am I, Amanda?*

I don't know, David, more normal? Now the last
one goes by. The last woman also passes, and before
she follows the children she stands looking at me for
a moment. I open the car door. Everything starts to
go white. I can't stop rubbing my eyes because it feels
like I have something in them.

*It feels like worms.*

Yes. If I had water I could wash my face. I get out
and lean against the car. I think about the women.

*The nurses.*

"Mommy . . ." Nina is crying.

Maybe if they could give me a little water, but it's

so hard to think, David. I'm so dazed and I'm so thirsty and so anxious and Nina calls to me nonstop, and I can't look at her, now I can't see practically anything. There is white on all sides, and now I'm the one calling Nina. I feel my way along the car and I try to get back in.

"Nina. Nina," I cry out.

Everything is white. Nina's hands touch my face and I push them away harshly.

"Nina," I say. "Ring the doorbell of a house. Ring the bell and tell them to call Daddy."

Nina, I say over and over, many times. But where is Nina now, David? How could I be without Nina all this time? David, where is she?

*Carla came to see you as soon as she found out they'd brought you back to the emergency clinic. Seven hours passed between when you fainted and when Carla came to* visit, and over a day since the moment you were poisoned. *Carla thinks it is all related to the children in the waiting room, to the death of the horses, the dog, and the ducks, and to the son who is no longer her son but who goes on living in her house. Carla believes it is all her fault, that changing me that afternoon from one body to another body has changed something else. Something small and invisible that has ruined everything.*

And is it true?

*This isn't her fault. It's something much worse.*

And Nina?

*Carla came right away, and when she saw that you were so feeble, sweating with fever, and that you were hallucinating me, she was convinced that the important thing was to talk to the woman in the green house.*

It's true, she's sitting at the foot of the bed, and she says talking to the woman in the green house is the best thing we can do. Now she wants to know if I agree. What is she talking about, David?

*Do you see her? Can you see now, again?*

I see a little, it's all very white still but my eyes aren't burning now. Did they give me something to calm the burning? I see blurry shapes, I recognize your mother's form, her voice. I tell her to call my husband, and Carla practically runs to me. She grabs my hands, she asks me how I am.

"Call my husband, Carla."

I tell her, I really did tell her.

*And she calls him. You say the number several times until she can get it down, she manages to find him, and she hands you a phone.*

Yes, it's his voice, finally it's his voice, and I'm crying so much that he can't understand what is happening. I am very sick, I realize, and I tell him. David, this is not sunstroke. And I can't stop crying, so much crying that he yells at me over the phone, he orders me to stop, to explain what is happening. He asks about Nina. Where is Nina, David?

*Then Carla takes the phone away from you, gently, and she tries to talk with your husband. She feels embarrassed, she doesn't really know what to say.*

She says that I'm not well, that there are no doctors in the emergency clinic today but they've sent for one. She asks my husband if he'll come. She says yes, that Nina is fine. You see, David, you see that Nina is fine. Carla is very close now. Where are you? Does your mother know you're with me?

*She wouldn't be surprised if she knew; she tells herself that I'm behind all of these things. That whatever has cursed this town for the past ten years is now inside me.*

She sits on the bed, very close. Again, the sweet

perfume of her sunscreen. She smooths my hair, and her fingers are icy but her touch is pleasant. And the noise of her bracelets. Do I have a high fever, David?

"Amanda," your mother says.

I think she is crying, there is something halting in her voice when she pronounces my name. She insists on calling the woman in the green house. She says there's not much time.

*She's right.*

"We have to do it fast," she says, and she holds my hands, her cold hands squeeze mine, soaking wet, and she caresses my wrists. "Tell me you agree, I need your consent."

I think she wants to bring me to the green house.

"I'll stay in my body, Carla."

I don't believe in those things, I want to tell her. But it seems like that's something she's unable to hear.

"Amanda, I don't mean you, I mean Nina," your mother says. "As soon as I heard they'd brought you here I asked about Nina, but no one knew where she was. We went looking for her in Mr. Geser's car."

The rope pulls tighter.

*She was sitting on the curb, a few blocks past where they parked your car.*

"Amanda, when I find my real David," your mother says, "I won't have any doubt it's him." She squeezes my hands very tightly, as if I were going to fall over from one moment to the next. "You have to understand that Nina wasn't going to make it many more hours."

"Where is Nina?" I ask again, frantically. Hundreds of needles of pain radiate from my throat to the extremities of my body.

Your mother isn't asking for my consent. Your

mother is asking for my forgiveness, for what is happening right now, in the green house. I let go of her hands. The rescue distance knots up, so brutally that for a moment I stop breathing. I think about leaving, about getting out of bed. My God, I think. My God. I have to get Nina out of that house.

*But it will be a while before you can move. The effect comes and goes, the fever comes and goes.*

I have to talk to my husband again. I have to tell him where Nina is. The pain comes back, it's a white blow to the head, intermittent, blinding me for seconds at a time.

"Amanda . . ." says Carla.

"No, no." I say no, over and over.

*Too many times.*

Am I shouting?

*Nina's name.*

Carla tries to hug me and it's hard to push her away. My body heats up to an unbearable temperature, my fingers swell up under my nails.

*But you don't stop shouting, and one of the nurses is in the room now.*

She talks to Carla. What does she say, David, what does she say?

*That a doctor is on the way.*

But there's no hope for me now.

*The pain comes and goes, the fever comes and goes, and there is Carla again, holding your hands.*

I see Nina's hands, for a moment. She's not here but I see them with utter clarity. Her little hands are dirty with mud.

*Or they're my dirty hands when I came into the kitchen, and without letting go of the wall, I looked for Carla from the threshold.*

That's not true, they're Nina's hands, I can see them.

"It was what had to be done," says Carla.

It's happening now. Why are Nina's hands covered in mud? What do my daughter's hands smell like?

"No, Carla. No, please."

The ceiling moves farther away and my body sinks into the darkness of the bed.

"I need to know where she's going," I say.

When Carla leans over me, everything is in complete silence.

"That can't happen, Amanda. I already told you that can't happen."

The blades of the ceiling fan move slowly and the air doesn't reach me.

"You have to ask the woman," I say.

"But Amanda . . ."

"You have to beg her."

Someone approaches, from the hallway. The footsteps are so soft, almost imperceptible, but I can hear them precisely. Like your steps in the green house, two little wet feet on the splintered wood.

"Tell her to try to leave Nina as close as possible."

Can you intervene, David? Can you leave Nina close?

*Close to whom?*

Close, close to home.

*I could.*

Whatever it takes, please.

*I could, but it won't do any good.*

Please, David. And that's the last thing I can say, I know it is the last thing, I know it a second before I say it. Everything is silent, finally. A long and tonal silence. Now there are no blades or ceiling fan. Now there is no nurse. Carla is gone. The sheets aren't here, nor the bed, nor the room. Things are no longer happening. Only my body is here. David?

*What?*

I'm so tired. What is the important thing, David? I need you to say it, because the ordeal is ending, right? I need you to say it, and then I want everything to stay quiet.

*I'm going to push you now. I push the ducks, I push Mr. Geser's dog, and the horses.*

And the girl from House & Home. Is this about the poison? It's everywhere, isn't it, David?

*The poison was always there.*

Is it about something else, then? Is it because I did something wrong? Was I a bad mother? Is it something I caused? The rescue distance.

*The pain comes and goes.*

When Nina and I were on the lawn, among the barrels. It was the rescue distance: it didn't work, I didn't see the danger. And now there is something else in my body, something that activates again or maybe it deactivates, something sharp and bright.

*It's the pain.*

Why don't I feel it anymore?

*It pierces the stomach.*

Yes, it bores in and rips it open, but I don't feel it. It reaches me with a cold, white vibration, it reaches my eyes.

*I'm touching your hands, I'm right here.*

And now the rope, the rope of the rescue distance.

*Yes.*

It's as if it were tied to my stomach from outside. It pulls tight.

*Don't be scared.*

It's crushing, David.

*It's going to break.*

No, that can't happen. The rope cannot break, because I am Nina's mother and Nina is my daughter.

*Did you ever think about my father?*

Your father? Something pulls harder at the rope and it tightens around my stomach. It's going to slice my stomach in two.

*It will break first. Breathe.*

This rope can't break, Nina is my daughter. But yes, my God, it's broken.

*Now there is very little time left.*

Am I dying?

*Yes. There are seconds left, but you could still understand the important thing. I'm going to push you ahead so you can listen to my father.*

Why your father?

*He seems rough and simple to you, but that's because he is a man who has lost his horses.*

Something falls away.

*The rope.*

There is no more tension. But I feel the rope, it still exists.

*Yes, but there's not much time left. There will be only a few seconds of clarity. When my father speaks, don't get distracted.*

Your voice is weak, I can't hear you very well now.

*Pay attention, Amanda, it will last only a few seconds. Do you see something now?*

It's my husband.

*I'm pushing you forward. Do you see?*

Yes.

*This is going to be the last effort. This is the last thing that will happen.*

Yes, I see him. It's my husband, he's driving our car. He's entering the town now. Is this really happening?

*Don't interrupt the story.*

I see him clear and bright.

*Don't turn back.*

It's my husband.

*At the end, I won't be here anymore.*

But David . . .

*Don't waste any more time talking to me.*

He takes the boulevard and drives slowly forward. I see everything so clearly. The stoplight is red and he stops. It's the town's only stoplight, and two old people cross the street and look at him. But he is distracted, he looks forward, he doesn't take his eyes from the road. He passes the plaza, the supermarket, and the service station. He passes the emergency clinic. He takes the gravel road, to the right. He

drives slowly and in a straight line. He doesn't drive
around the potholes, or the small speed bumps. Beyond the town, Mr. Geser's dogs come running out
and bark at the tires, but he maintains his speed. He
passes the house I rented with Nina. He doesn't look
at it. He leaves the house behind, and then Carla's
house comes into view. He takes the dirt road and
goes up the hill. He leaves the car next to the trees
and turns the motor off. He opens the car door. He is
aware of how loud things are: when he closes the
door, the slam echoes back from the fields. He looks
at the dirty old house, the places where the roof was
mended with tin. Behind it the sky is dark, and
though it's noon, some lights are on inside. He is nervous, and he knows someone might be watching him.
Still without going up the three wooden steps, he
looks at the open door and the plastic curtain tied

across it. A small bell hangs from the roof, but he doesn't pull the rope that hangs from it. Instead he knocks twice, and from inside a deep voice says, "Come in." A man the same age as him is in the kitchen; he is looking for something in the cupboards and he pays no attention to my husband. It's Omar, your father, but they don't seem to know each other.

"May I speak with you?" asks my husband.

Your father doesn't answer, and my husband chooses not to ask again. He starts to move closer, but he hesitates a moment. The kitchen is small and the man doesn't move. My husband takes a step onto the damp wood floor, which creaks. Something in the man's immobility makes my husband think this is not the first visit he has received.

"Would you like some *mate*?" your father asks, his back already turned as he dumps the used *yerba* into the sink. My husband says yes. Your father points to one of the chairs, and he sits down.

"I hardly even met your wife," says your father. He sticks two fingers into the *mate* gourd and throws the remaining *yerba* away.

"But your wife met her," says my husband.

"My wife is gone."

He puts the gourd on the table. He doesn't slam it down, but it is not a friendly movement, either. He places the *yerba* and the sugar on the table, then sits down across from my husband and looks at him.

"Go ahead," he says.

Hanging on the wall behind him, there are two pictures of the man with the same woman, and below are more photos of the man with various horses. A single nail holds them all up. Each picture hangs from the previous one, each tied with the same thin rope.

"My daughter is not well," says my husband. "It's been more than a month, but . . ."

Your father doesn't look at him, and pours another *mate*.

"I mean, she's doing okay, they're treating her and the spots on her skin don't hurt as much anymore. She's recovering, in spite of all she's been through. But there's something else, and I don't know what it is. Something more, within her." A few seconds pass before he goes on, as if he wanted to give your father time to take in his words. "Do you know what happened, what happened to Nina?"

"No."

There is a moment of silence, very long, during which neither of the two moves.

"You must know."

"I don't know."

My husband slams his hands down on the table, contained but effective. The sugar bowl jumps and its lid falls a little to the side. Now your father does look at him, but he speaks without fear.

"You know there's nothing I can tell you."

Your father brings the straw to his mouth. It's the only object that shines in the kitchen. My husband is going to say something else. But then there is a noise, it's coming from the hallway. Something is happening that my husband, from where he's sitting, can't see. Something familiar for the other man, who isn't alarmed. It's you, David. There's something different that I couldn't begin to describe, but it's you. You peer into the kitchen and stand there looking at them. My husband looks at you, his fists relax, he tries to calculate your age. He focuses on your strange gaze, which at certain moments strikes him as dim-witted; he notices your spots.

"There you have it," says your father, pouring another *mate* and again not offering any to my husband. "As you can see, I would also like to have someone to ask."

You wait quietly, attentive to my husband.

"And now he's started tying everything."

Your father points toward the living room, where many more things are hanging from rope, or are tied together with it. Now my husband's whole attention is focused on that, though he couldn't say why. It doesn't seem like a disproportionate number of things. It seems more like, in your own way, you were trying to do something with the deplorable state of the house and everything in it. My husband looks at you again, trying to understand, but you run out through the front door, and the two men are left in silence to listen to your steps moving away from the house.

"Come," says your father.

They get up almost at the same time. My husband follows him outside. He sees him glance to both sides as he goes down the steps, maybe looking for you. He sees your father as a tall and strong man, he sees his large hands hanging down at his sides, open. He stops, not far from the house. My husband takes a few steps toward him. They are close together, close and at the same time alone in so much open land. Beyond the soy fields it looks green and bright under the dark clouds. But the ground they are walking on, from the road to the stream, is dry and hard.

"You know," says your father, "I used to work with

horses." He shakes his head, maybe to himself. "But do you hear my horses now?"

"No."

"Do you hear anything else?"

Your father looks around, as if he can hear the silence much farther away than my husband is capable of hearing. The air smells of rain and a damp breeze wafts up from the ground.

"You need to go," says your father.

My husband nods as if grateful for the instruction, or the permission.

"If it starts to rain you'll get stuck in the mud, you won't get out."

They walk together toward the car, now with more distance between them. Then my husband sees you. You're sitting in the backseat. Your head barely clears the backrest. My husband approaches and looks in through the driver's-side window, determined to make you get out. He wants to leave right now. Upright against the seat, you look him in the eyes, as though begging him. I see through my husband, I see those other eyes in yours. The seat belt on, legs crossed on the seat. A hand reaching slightly toward Nina's stuffed mole, covertly, the dirty fingers resting on the stuffed legs as if trying to restrain them.

"Get out, please," says my husband. "Get out right now."

"As if he were going somewhere," says your father, opening the back door of the car.

Eyes desperately seek out my husband's gaze. But your father unclasps the seat belt and pulls you out by the arm. My husband gets into the car, furious, while the two figures walk away, return to the house, distant. First one enters, then the other, and the door closes from inside. Only then does my husband start the car, drive down the hill, and take the gravel road. He feels like he's already wasted enough time. He doesn't stop in town. He doesn't look back. He doesn't see the soy fields, the streams that crisscross the dry plots of land, the miles of open fields empty of livestock, the tenements and the factories as he reaches the city. He doesn't notice that the return trip has grown slower and slower. That there are too many cars, cars and more cars covering every asphalt nerve. Or that the transit is stalled, paralyzed for hours, smoking and effervescent. He doesn't see the important thing: the rope finally slack, like a lit fuse, somewhere; the motionless scourge about to erupt.

## About the Author

Samanta Schweblin was chosen by *Granta* as one of the twenty-two best writers in Spanish under the age of thirty-five. She is the author of three story collections, which have won numerous awards, including the prestigious Juan Rulfo Prize, and been translated into twenty languages. *Fever Dream* is her first novel and is a finalist for the Mario Vargas Llosa Prize and winner of the Tigre Juan Prize. Originally from Buenos Aires, she lives in Berlin.

## About the Translator

Megan McDowell is a literary translator from Kentucky who has translated many contemporary authors from Latin America and Spain, including Alejandro Zambra. She lives in Chile.